Th[ey Died]
in vain

Overlooked, Underappreciated and Forgotten Mystery Novels

edited by Jim Huang

A Drood Review Book

THE CRUM CREEK PRESS

Carmel, Indiana

Acknowledgments

The editor would like to acknowledge the invaluable assistance of Jeanne Jacobson, Jennie Jacobson and Beth Thoenen in the preparation of this book.

They Died in Vain

ISBN: 0-9625804-7-3

Cover art by Robin Agnew (Aunt Agatha's, Ann Arbor, MI)

First edition: April 2002

The Crum Creek Press
c/o The Drood Review
484 East Carmel Drive #378
Carmel, IN 46032

www.droodreview.com

Contents

Introduction 4

Part I • They Died in Vain 6
Essays on overlooked, underappreciated and forgotten mystery novels, personal favorites of genre booksellers, reviewers and devotees.

Part II • Contributors 168
Biographical notes about the contributors to this volume, including contact information for contributors' businesses.

Appendix • Shopping list 186
A checklist, including current publication information to make shopping easy.

Introduction

As mystery fans, we share affection for many well-known books — longtime favorites, widely-recognized classics, new books by bestselling writers. But this genre's rich and diverse history includes thousands of other great books, favorites of devotees who are eager to have you share their passion, eager for you to discover their buried treasures.

In this guide, we go beyond the bestsellers, beyond the familiar, in 103 essays, each of which will introduce you to a mystery you may not know about yet. Given the often whimsical vagaries of book promotion and distribution, it's no surprise that many mysteries fail to find their audience. I've been working in this field for nearly 20 years and I've read mysteries for many more, but as I put together this book, I've learned about books that I'd never heard about before.

They Died in Vain grows out of my work on the Independent Mystery Booksellers Association's list of 100 favorite mysteries of the twentieth century. It's a great list, and it's served to refocus attention on these cherished classics. Perhaps the most unexpected but nevertheless entertaining and valuable byproduct of IMBA's effort has been all the talk about the great mysteries that are not included among the IMBA 100. I acknowledged some of this conversation in our book, *100 Favorite Mysteries of the Century* (2000), by inviting contributing booksellers to list five books that "did not make the final list, but should have" — their responses are a delight.

But that didn't end the conversation, and it's not limited to booksellers either. Reviews of our 100 favorites book continue to cite omissions, other favorites that reviewers wanted their readers to know about. At conventions, on email discussion lists, whenever I've spoken to fans, to librarians, to bookselling colleagues and to fellow reviewers, I keep hearing enthusiastic comments about more great mysteries.

The book that you're holding in your hands is the result.

Our methodology was simple. I asked mystery booksellers, reviewers for various fan publications and others who are a part of this genre's remarkable and dedicated fan infrastructure to write about no more than two favorites among mysteries that they felt were overlooked, underappreciated or forgotten. The only criteria that was that each author could be represented only once in this book, and that these titles could not be bestsellers, although some of these authors' other titles are bestsellers. We feel sure that several of the up-and-coming authors discussed here will soon hit the bestseller lists.

The selections are idiosyncratic and personal. These books span the history of the genre, with original publication dates ranging from 1878 through 2000, and range from comfortable cozies to challenging whodunits to intricate procedurals to intense suspense — something for every mystery reader.

The 103 essays in this volume are organized alphabetically by the author of the book covered. In the section following the essays are biographical notes about the contributors, including contact information for many of the contributors' periodicals, bookselling or other businesses. Finally, we've put together a checklist that includes current publication information for each title featured in this book.

Our selections haven't necessarily received the attention they deserve, the marketplace may have passed them by (53 are not longer in print, some of these unavailable titles just a few years old), or they've been forgotten. Except, of course, in the hearts and minds of the essayists included here.

We invite you to rediscover these gems. You'll see that — to paraphrase the immortal words of Lina Lamont — the deaths of these characters ain't been in vain for nothing.

Happy reading!

— *Jim Huang*

They Died in Vain

The Stately Home Murder by Catherine Aird (1969)
aka The Complete Steel

Happily for avid readers of sly and witty cozies, Kinn Hamilton McIntosh (aka Catherine Aird) is still writing her contemporary police procedural mysteries, set in the Trollopian county of West Calleshire, England.

Anthony Trollope followed Thomas Hardy's idea of creating an imaginary county for his series. This idea was later wickedly continued by Angela Thirkell in her own Barsetshire novels; Aird took up this conceit and has made Berebury her capital and West Calleshire her own literary fiefdom.

Aird is a master of ingenious methods of killing someone with innocuous objects, beginning in her first book in the series, *The Religious Body* (1966), with an unscrewed finial from a staircase's newel post as the murder weapon, to a full-figured statue in a locked tower in *His Burial Too*.

Lovers of English and traditional mysteries will find each story contains a sly tweaking of one or more of the murder mystery conventions, and what a wonderful joke Aird has in store for the reader at the end of *The Stately Home Murder*!

In *The Stately Home Murder*, the landed aristocracy is struggling to stay alive despite vicious onslaughts from the Inland Revenue without and from murder within. Readers are led on a witty romp through a world inhabited by dotty great-aunts, a butterfly-witted Countess and rapscallion scions of the house, and they will enjoy the pleasures of touring a stately mansion in too-tight shoes only to find the body of the desiccated family archivist.

This unfortunate gentleman was pointedly disinvited to tea with the great-aunts and then battered to death with a medieval club (in the library) after discovering a document suggesting the current Earl is not entitled to the title.

As Inspector C.D. Sloan reports to his superior "'we're a bit spoilt by choice of weapons, sir, not counting two small cannon at the front door'" — one hundred seventy-seven to be exact. The body was discovered in "Grumpy," one of eight suits of armor in the Armaments Room.

The names of the medieval weaponry fly around the imperturbable Sloan, but despite wishing crime would stop while his roses are in bloom, he doggedly follows all leads and after another body is found — in the dank oubliette this time — Sloan gets his murderer.

Inspector C.D. Sloan is the harassed and engaging glue that holds this series together, supported by his gormless sidekick (there's never anyone else available, alas) Crosby, and their unpleasant superintendent, Leeyes — reminiscent of Richard Jury's superior, Race, in Martha Grimes' mysteries. Aird adds a fillip to Leeyes as in each book he has just become an expert in a new and peculiar subject, used to great effect to plague his officers.

As for Crosby, he is a wonderful foil for the patient Sloan. In *Stately Home*, the first murder weapon was a godentag club, literally a "good morning." As the inimitable Crosby points out: "'If that's what did it, sir, shouldn't it be "Good Night?"'"

Catherine Aird has written eighteen novels in the West Calleshire series. Her latest, *Little Knell,* was published in England in 2000.

Josephine Bayne

Night Dogs by Kent Anderson (1996)

Night Dogs is a gripping and emotionally draining episodic tale of a police officer on the job.

Officer Hanson and his partner, Dana, patrol the North

Precinct, a poor and mostly black section of Portland, Oregon in the mid 1970s. There is no major crime for these officers to solve. No serial killer is running amok within their patrol area. Instead, we ride with Hanson and Dana from call to call, from one near-tragedy to another, from the routine calls that show their difficult position in a hostile neighborhood to the near-explosive calls where the officers are confronted by Muslims there to "observe" the police work. Most of the cops are white, the territory is black, and *Night Dogs* again and again reveals the "us against them," white versus black mentality. The parallels between Hanson's Special Forces Vietnam experience and his job in the North District — that these are both wars where there is an occupying force that is distrusted by the indigenous population, that it's all about survival — are drawn repeatedly. It's like Vietnam, Hanson explains; "Anyone you didn't know, or trust, you killed."

We don't know a lot about Hanson, where he came from, or why — other than Vietnam — he is the way he is. Troubled, isolated and unsettled, he is not averse to taking the occasional toot to smooth things out. His friends are his partner and fellow officers, as well as the only surviving member of his Special Forces team, Doc, a local criminal who eventually commits a terrible, unforgivable crime. His confidante is Truman, a blind little dog he saved from the pound. He cares for this dog, and his conversations with Truman are the only soft spots in this whole gritty book.

Not surprisingly, the physically and emotionally isolated Hanson has difficulties with personal relationships. His forays into the dating world are clumsy and don't go well. In one scene, he is invited to a party and wonders to himself whether, if he had to, he could kill the seven or eight people there with just the nine bullets in his gun. Probably not, he concludes, because he would have to do mostly head shots and people would start running. It would be easier to make them all lie down and execute them. Sure, let's invite this guy to the next party.

Hanson is war- and job-weary. But he is also professional, compassionate and understanding, unrelentingly dedicated to his work. "I've found my community… They hate me there, but that's okay, that's my job in the community. To be hated. I know where I stand." Ultimately, he is too good for the job.

This book is not for those who like their heroes clean and virtuous. It is also unabashedly pro-police. You feel for them, worry as they approach dangerous situations, and watch as they cleanly de-escalate confrontations. This is a wonderful and frightening book.

Kent Anderson wrote *Night Dogs* in 1996 as the second in a trilogy, following *Sympathy for the Devil* which came out ten years earlier. Originally published in a very small printing, it was re-released a year later by Bantam. Like his protagonist, Anderson was a Portland police officer for three years and served with the Special Forces in Vietnam. James Crumley wrote the terrific foreword.

Joseph Morales

Death from the Woods by Brigitte Aubert (2000)
Translated by David L. Koral

Given a protagonist who is quadriplegic, blind and mute, the prospect of creating a detective thriller seems daunting. In the capable hands of Brigitte Aubert, it becomes a tour de force.

Elise Andioli's mind has in no way been diminished by the terrorist bomb that robbed her not only of her fiancée but of speech, sight and movement. The 36-year-old is ill-suited to her disabilities having, by her own admission, been physically active, sharp-tongued and outspoken before the catastrophe. "I used to ski, play tennis, go walking and swimming. I liked the sun, going for drives, traveling, and reading novels about love. Now I'm buried inside myself and every day I pray to die completely."

Except for her doctor and Yvette, her caregiver, people tend to behave around Elise as if she were invisible or senile. Until Virginie. Virginie is seven years old. She meets Elise outside the local supermarket where Yvette has parked Elsie while she shops. With the clear logic of a child, Virginie divines a way of communicating, in a very limited way, with Elise — through Elise's one mobile part, one finger. A raised finger means "yes." No finger raised, "no." Virginie shares a secret with Elise. She knows about the children who are being murdered. She knows the murderer. Well, that opens Elise's ears. The gossip between Yvette and the masseuse and events reported on the evening news take on a whole new dimension. "I'm surrounded by big blabber-mouths. They're addicted to conversation. Now, isn't that a blessing!"

In no time Elise is transformed from a woman willing herself to die to a woman taken out of her self-involved depression and given a purpose — to find a way to help Virginie. In her condition, what can Elise do to unmask the murderer and protect Virginie? For a start, she listens and hears more than people realize they are saying. And, through Virginie's interest in her, she begins to have visitors — Virginie's parents, who introduce her to some of their friends and, more importantly, Captain Yssart from the murder squad who may be her answer to helping Virginie. The progress of her investigation will keep you enthralled to the last page as Aubert builds her story to a terrifying climax.

Aubert's writing is fluid with an almost poetic grace, which must be a credit to the translator, David L. Koral, for preserving the essence of her prose from the original French. Since all of the descriptions are filtered through Elise, she relies on her memories of people as they were before her accident.

This is a "locked person" mystery, as we are confined to the narrative of Elise's mind. "I'm what you call a quadriplegic. And as if I weren't happy enough to lose the use of my limbs, then I really hit the jackpot when I lost my sight and ability to speak..." Aubert creates a protagonist who is believable despite her infirmities and builds the suspense to an unbearable pitch.

You will not forget this story, nor its heroine.

Aubert is a well-known crime writer in France. *Death from the Woods* and its sequel, *Snow from the Woods*, provide American readers with the opportunity to discover this talented author.

Sally Powers

Death's Favorite Child by Frankie Y. Bailey (2000)

Criminologist and professor Lizzie Stuart is ready for a vacation after the death of her beloved grandmother. Having spent the better part of her life in a small town in Kentucky, she decides to go someplace totally different and plans a week in St. Regis, a resort town in Cornwall, with her best friend, Tess, a travel writer.

In short order, Lizzie is convinced by Tess's ex-husband, Michael, to deliver a present to Tess, is pushed and nearly run down by a London bus, witnesses a murder in St. Regis and finds herself in danger of being the next victim. Detective John Quinn from Philadelphia is also visiting the resort town, and he and Lizzie pool their talents to solve the crime, with the somewhat reluctant approval of the Cornish police. In the meantime, Lizzie is confused by just what the relationship between Tess and Michael might be, seven years after their divorce, and why Tess is behaving rather oddly. Lizzie never cared much for Michael in the past and still doesn't, but she wants her friend to be happy. Then there are the other visitors in the small hotel, as well as the staff and some of the townspeople, all of whom add to the puzzle of who wanted to kill Dee, housekeeper at the hotel and niece of the owners.

Nearly everything about *Death's Favorite Child* is just a little bit more than the reader might expect, leading me to choose this as my favorite mystery of 2000. It's a cross between the traditional cozy and police procedural, the protagonists are American in a British mystery and Lizzie is the only African-American. All the characters are memorable and there is a good balance between plot and character development. The potential relationship between Lizzie and John is intriguing, particularly in light of their many differences.

Frankie Y. Bailey is herself a criminologist and university professor. She is the author of several nonfiction works and her writing skills are well-honed. *Death's Favorite Child* is her first mystery, followed by *A Dead Man's Honor* in 2001, this one set in Virginia where Lizzie is a visiting professor.

When I first met Frankie, she was sitting at a signing table at a mystery convention but her newly-released book wasn't available because only a handful had arrived in time. Shrugging off a disappointing situation, she was using her time to talk to people and tell them about her book. It sounded very appealing and when she told me she grew up in Virginia and often spends time here, I was determined to read it. I will be forever be grateful to Frankie for giving me and other mystery readers such pleasure.

Lelia Taylor

Complicity by Iain Banks (1995)

I decide: When in doubt it's vitally important to keep moving. Velocity is important. Kinetic energy frees the brain and confuses the enemy.

If any author can claim to be an authority on kinetic verbal energy, it's the prolific and bizarre Iain Banks. Banks writes both fiction *(The Wasp Factory)* and science fiction *(Consider Phlebas),* and has a rabid cult following among readers of both genres. He's beloved by his fans for many reasons, chief among them the sheer originality of his mind.

Complicity is a whodunit that begins in the second person, putting us behind the eyes of a killer: "You hear the car after an hour and a half. During that time you've been here in the darkness, sitting on the small telephone seat near the front door, waiting." This device immediately blurs the lines between ourselves and the criminal; no one is completely innocent here, not even us as readers.

The story follows Cameron Colley, a Scottish newspaper writer, whose normal routine (drugs, booze, computer games, and a hot and sweaty affair with a married college friend) is disrupted when he becomes a suspect in a string of extremely brutal attacks and slayings. All of these crimes are truly horrifying, not least for their aptness: a judge who released suspected rapists is raped; a child pornographer is injected with a syringe full of semen. Cameron becomes a suspect for reasons that may or may not be purely circumstantial. He not only must unravel the mystery on a literal level, but also is forced into spiritual self-examination, as long-repressed memories surface and his previously blurry life snaps into painfully sharp focus.

Moral issues knot themselves around the heart of *Complicity*, enough to power a university ethics seminar. Where is the dividing line between justice and revenge? When do games of trust become sadistic? Why is it so difficult to separate the moral from the political, and the emotional from the physical? Banks plays with all these questions gleefully, and though readers may want to look away, we — you — can't.

Banks has said that *Complicity,* which is set in the early 1990s, is his response to the horror of the Thatcher years. He sometimes falls into the trap of speechifying through his characters, and is most effective when he's at his least polemical. But if the book were only a cry of anger, it would not be useful or interesting. Banks has woven his disgust into a tapestry of rage, given form to his fury.

Complicity is a mystery in the same primordial sense as

David Lynch's movies or Haruki Murakami's short stories. They're all as mysterious as life, and make sense at some subcellular level we can't turn away from or deny. Banks has the added benefit of being an excellent plotter and avoiding the almost inevitable anticlimax — once we figure out who the killer is, we still wonder, what the hell happens now?

Mysteries should challenge the mind, and the question of whodunit should be secondary to those of why it was done, and so what. Banks is brave enough to go way out on a limb, and his efforts pay off here. *Complicity* is at once education, assault and entertainment.

Anya Weber

Death and Other Lovers by Jo Bannister (1991)

Jo Bannister is a sadly underappreciated writer, a master of sharp characterization, unexpected humor and telling detail. *Death and Other Lovers* partakes of those strengths, and has one of the most elegant plots I've ever encountered. It is a thing of startling twists and breathtaking symmetry, both beautiful and utterly satisfying.

Photographer Mickey Flynn knows someone is trying to kill him. His apartment is torched and then a bomb planted in his suitcase blows a plane out of the sky — a plane that he was on until minutes before it took off. Flynn identifies four men whom he has harmed or offended so badly that they might want to kill him, and sets about confronting them: a drug lord, a politician, a mercenary and a Palestinian militant.

Bannister is a journalist, and her descriptions of Flynn's exploits in photographic journalism are fascinating. Best of all is a subtle, brilliantly conceived smear campaign against the drug lord, who is eventually routed from his cover of respectability and forced to flee to Colombia. A sample:

In New York Flynn photographed the [drug lord's] long white car outside a lawyer's office. The ostensible subject of the picture was some street theatre. On the same page was news that the lawyer had been retained to defend two men accused of breaking legs in a dispute over who should sell what drugs on which street corner.

In Washington Flynn photographed the long white car in traffic alongside a delivery van for a ... pharmaceuticals outlet. Both vehicles had been held up for the parade that was the alleged focus of the picture. But the placement of the caption describing it had necessitated cropping most of the van's side panel ... Only the word "druggist" hung over the white car like an accusation.

Flynn's emotional experience is particularly well drawn. As he walks away from disaster after disaster, then confronts his enemies and still lives to tell about it, Flynn develops a kind of despairing sense of immortality meshed with survivor's guilt that rings true and wrings the heart. Bannister picked up on this emotional thread when she chose as an epigraph for *Death and Other Lovers* a portion of Robert Southey's *The Curse of Kehama*:

...And thou shalt seek Death
To release thee, in vain;
Thou shalt live in thy pain
While Kehama shall reign,
With a fire in thy heart,
And a fire in thy brain;
And Sleep shall obey me,
And visit thee never,
And the Curse shall be on thee
For ever and ever.

But it's the plot, which twists startlingly at the halfway point and again at the end, that makes this book stand out.

Death and Other Lovers is the sequel to a novel published under two titles, *Critical Angle* and *Shards*. Bannister also writes four series: the excellent Castlemere books, which begin with *A Bleeding of Innocents* and feature a trio of police detectives; the Primrose Holland books, about an advice columnist, starting with *The Primrose Convention*; the Dr. Clio Rees series, which begins with another two-titled book — *Striving with Gods* was also published as *Uncertain Death*; and a new series beginning with *Echoes of Lies*, published in the US in 2001.

Beth Thoenen

A Trouble of Fools by Linda Barnes (1987)

A Trouble of Fools begins the ultimate Boston mystery series, featuring 6'1", red-haired private eye and part-time hack driver Carlotta Carlyle. Right from the beginning you can feel Carlotta is a part of Boston. When Carlotta drives around, the city pulses with life as Linda Barnes details the different (from Harvard Square to Southie) and how they connect. You get a sense of the vitality of the city and the social conflicts between ethnic groups. Carlotta herself has a history, a network of friends, and she lives for more than catching bad guys (volleyball and blues guitar are her hobbies).

Barnes introduces a supporting cast that will keep Carlotta company through seven more titles: her wacky artist tenant Roz, old police force boss Mooney, cab dispatcher Gloria, on-again off-again lover Sam Gianelli and Little Sister Paolina. They are each important for reflecting a different part of Carlotta's personality. Roz is the unofficial sidekick, injecting humor and helping with the grunt work. Mooney is Carlotta's police contact and keeps her working in the bounds of the law. Gloria is the one with contacts and information; being overweight and wheelchair-bound disguises her intellect and strength. Gianelli is mysterious and full of trouble; Carlotta can't resist their sexual chemistry. Paolina is like a daughter and keeps Carlotta compassionate. These characters grow (having highs and lows) just as much as Carlotta does over the series.

In *Trouble of Fools*, Gloria refers investigation business to Carlotta in the form of Margaret Devens, sister to missing old-time cabbie Eugene. Margaret doesn't want to go to the police and Eugene's buddies at the cab company are tight-lipped about his whereabouts. So Carlotta goes undercover in her old job to search for clues. Each night she follows a different cabbie. Persistence pays off as she finds the cronies gathered for beers and gab at an Irish bar in Brighton. While following the trail, Carlotta uncovers a scheme involving the IRA and drugs. Carlotta's resolution ties up neatly with a problem at Paolina's school and Carlotta's quest to claim a $20,000 prize for Thomas C. Carlyle, her cat.

A Trouble of Fools is a favorite of mine because of Carlotta. Here's a single woman who's had bumps in her life and is doing okay. She's survived a marriage wrecked by drugs, she's survived an abbreviated career in the police force, she's survived shoes that are not big enough. She's forged a strong relationship with Paolina, she has hobbies that give her an outlet for stress, she's grounded and interesting and funny. And if that isn't enough, Barnes gives us Boston and all its quirks.

Deb Tomaselli

Done Wrong by Eleanor Taylor Bland (1995)

Eleanor Taylor Bland's series starring widowed African-American cop Marti MacAlister is a real find — insightful, well-written, complex, and confident. After the death of her cop husband, Marti and her two children moved to Lincoln Park, Illinois, where they share a house with her friend Sharon. In these books, real people cope with their real lives in real places that have weather, neighbors, pets and homework. However, this appealing picture of African-American middle-class life is threatened by the stress and dangers of Marti's work as well as the evil that may lie hidden beneath apparently placid surfaces.

Many of the books' titles suggest this theme of hidden danger: *Keep Still, See No Evil, Tell No Tales, Scream in Silence.* In *Keep Still,* a lonely old woman in the neighborhood falls — or is pushed — down the stairs; in *See No Evil,* Marti doesn't know that someone is stalking her daughter and sneaking into the house while everyone is away. (In one truly creepy scene, the intruder gives the family dog two extra-large Hershey bars. The comforting associations we have with chocolate make the malice of the act all the more unnerving.)

Lincoln Park also harbors more typical crime, of course, the drug deals, arson, child neglect, battered spouses, and corpses that call the police into action. Bland's handling of the criminal investigations is authentic in detail as well as feeling. She shows both the frustrations and the satisfactions of police work, the dead ends, the needle-in-a-haystack quality of so many investigations. She also displays acute social awareness, especially of the families destroyed by drugs and alcohol.

Characterization is one of Bland's greatest strengths. The relationship between Marti and her partner "Vic" Jessnovik is particularly well-drawn. In *Done Wrong*, they move off their suburban turf into Chicago, in order to investigate unresolved questions about the so-called suicide of Marti's husband Johnny. When Vic learns that Marti needs to find the truth and a sense of closure for herself and her children, his reaction is both simple and deeply moving: "What are we going to do?" With that "we," Bland shatters our stereotypical expectations about bigoted cops and conflicts over race and gender.

These intriguing police procedurals about real people and authentic police work aim for, and hit, a standard well above the norm. It's best to read them in order, since Marti's life evolves just as real lives do. We can follow as she works through her grief and anger over Johnny's death, develops a new love interest, and helps her children through the stages of growing up. For a multilayered and intelligent portrayal of life and crime as it really is, you won't be disappointed with Marti MacAlister and her world.

Patricia Davis

Working Murder by Eleanor Boylan (1989)

Some time after Elizabeth Daly's death, her niece Eleanor Boylan wrote five mysteries featuring Clara Gamadge, widow of Daly's sleuth Henry Gamadge (see page 40). Clara is 68 in the first installment and when I read these books I was delighted to discover an older woman, plagued by some of the obstacles of aging, carrying on a full and active life, and solving mysteries as well. She became, in a sense, my role model.

The first book in the series, *Working Murder*, begins less than a year after Henry's death. Clara has rented her home in New York and gone to Florida to stay with her good friend and cousin Charles Saddlier (Sadd). But she goes home again when she receives news that another cousin has died, initiating an intriguing drama involving a family mausoleum, all but empty, and a debutante who disappeared fifty years before. More will die before Clara reluctantly assumes Henry's role and uncovers the villain.

Working Murder is most definitely a cozy. There is no violence on stage at all. The characters are all related. Clara's sidekicks are Sadd and her son and daughter, Henry and Paula. It is nice to read about a family that gets along and is not dysfunctional. The fifty-year-old mystery is intriguing. All the elderly characters have known each other all their lives, and their world is the limited one of the socially eminent. All of them are nice people, even the villain.

19

Clara, as I mentioned, is growing old. She tires easily and her emotions frequently come to the surface. I must admit I got a little impatient because she often deferred to one of her male relatives and allowed him to tell her what to do. She gets over that in later books.

Boylan tells a good if limited story. The uncovering of the solution requires a certain leap of faith, but it works. She paints wonderful word pictures of the settings. I shall not forget the hulking mausoleum, snow all about it, other huge forms on every side, or the cold silent chapel, the only sound a child's fingers scrabbling for animal crackers. It is these scenes and the main character that make these books so attractive to me. The book was nominated for an Anthony Award for best first novel.

Boylan went on to write four more mysteries featuring Clara Gamadge. In *Murder Observed,* Clara is convinced that a divorced friend was deliberately run down and killed by a young man. This leads back to events that had happened before World War II. *Murder Machree* takes place mostly in Ireland. Two cousins both claim to be the same person and one of them is murdered. Clara is poisoned in *Pushing Murder* and must find out why. In the final book in the series, *Murder Crossed*, a down-at-the-heels actress dumps her three children with a childhood friend who is now head of the preparatory school that Clara attended, and then apparently gets murdered.

Sally Fellows

Hardly a Man is Now Alive by Herbert Brean (1950) aka Murder Now and Then

Before Jane Langton, before Amanda Cross, fans of witty, erudite puzzles could turn to Herbert Brean. Today, when remembered at all, Brean is remembered for *Wilders Walk Away* (1948), in which various members of the Wilder family down through the generations have simply disappeared. What seems unquestionably supernatural has a very earthbound solution, as our intrepid hero, photojournalist Reynold Frame, learns. But Brean couldn't let a good gimmick go, and repeated his magician's illusion several more times with various debunkers, including three more turns with Frame (*The Darker the Night* (1949), *The Clock Strikes Thirteen* (1952) and *Hardly a Man Is Now Alive*).

Hardly finds him headed for Concord, Massachusetts, one-time home to Louisa May Alcott, Nathaniel Hawthorne, Henry David Thoreau, Ralph Waldo Emerson, and the spirit of the American Revolution, all of which give the eclectic brilliance of Brean a chance to shine. Frame and Constance Wilder are on their wedding trip, but Frame needs to complete an assignment. Circumstances force him to room in a house rumored to be haunted by the ghost of the first British soldier killed in the Revolution. The first night's sleep isn't half over before Frame is confronted with some pretty strong evidence of the old stories. It isn't much longer before some more corporeal and contemporary remains are discovered in an old well. In the end, Frame solves a literary mystery, a kidnapping and two deaths, one nearly two centuries past.

Frame is a smart, funny, sometimes irascible, always thoroughly human protagonist who even seriously considers not reporting a dead body because it might delay his wedding plans. Characters, however, are not Brean's strong suit — that honor goes hands down to plot. And here, as a Miami Herald reviewer once said, we have a dilly. Deftly weaving political, military and literary history, Brean created a complex puzzle that offers all the necessary clues but does a very effective job of hiding them. One beguiling concept is that in 1950 one could hear a recounting of the opening moments of the Revolutionary War at second hand. Told by an elderly man who heard it as a child from a then-elderly man who had fought as a Minuteman (check it out — the numbers work without any suspension of disbelief), the story of the battle presents with an immediacy one won't get from any textbook, and forces the reader to confront the very essence of time.

Among the many other charms of Brean's books are footnotes that unabashedly interrupt the narrative: historical information, references to his other books, even — in this case — a recipe for Indian pudding! Each chapter begins with a quote from writers running the gamut from one of the Concord Minutemen to Sir Arthur Conan Doyle.

Brean wrote only seven mysteries during his long career as a writer, editor and newspaperman, each of which is a gem of clever diversion polished to a luster with a variety of fascinating facts.

Sue Feder

The Whispering Wall by Patricia Carlon (1969)

Imagine yourself paralyzed, unable to speak, but still with all your mental capacity. You are at the mercy of your caregivers and their words are cruel and careless as they believe you to be little more than a vegetable. Overhear a murder plot as another part of your predicament and you have Patricia Carlon's incredibly powerful suspense thriller, *The Whispering Wall.*

Stroke victim Sarah Oatland is confined to her bed, paralyzed and unable to speak. Gwenyth, her niece, has hired Nurse Bragg to oversee Sarah's daily care, but is really looking forward to Sarah's departure so she can inherit the coveted house. In the meantime, Gwenyth converts the downstairs into flats. One is rented to an overworked mother and her timid 11-year-old daughter, Rose. The other is taken by the Phippses; the husband smiles a bit too much and the wife is a bit too solicitous.

Murray and Valma Phipps are below Sarah's bedroom and Sarah hears them discuss plans to arrange a fatal accident for Valma's stepfather, old heartthrob singer Roderick Palmer. Sarah is determined to foil their plans, but how can she without tipping the Phippses off and putting herself in mortal danger?

The running conversation Sarah has with herself sustains her, keeps her focused to do her best to communicate and save a life. It is good that she is forgiving of what others say; they reveal themselves because of her incapacity. Rose and Roderick are the most kind. They treat Sarah like a person who has feelings and desires that have been quashed by her immobility. Nurse Bragg is committed to her duty, but forgets herself when she is not speaking to Sarah. She casually comments about Sarah being "laid out like a fish on a slab" in front of her. Gwenyth represents the greatest lack of sensitivity, openly declaring Sarah nothing more than a vegetable. She shows more concern for the property — it is more valuable to her. This attention to characterization runs strong in all Carlon's books and is a driving force in the suspense.

Carlon's books explore crime on a personal level. They take place within small neighborhoods and find conflict between the insiders and outsiders of the community. Carlon also demonstrates how crime affects family. Who to believe is something that changes between books, but the main perspective is from someone with little power, a single woman or child. These characters have to struggle to get help from others as their truthfulness usually gets questioned. Through common sense and a great desire for self preservation, the lead characters will themselves to succeed.

Carlon's books really make me feel: hatred of the bad guys, affection for the heroines, fear during the tense situations she's constructed. She explores the consequences of actions, and she shapes characters, places, and situations precisely. And she manages to do all this in usually under 200 pages. Carlon is a uniquely clever writer and *The Whispering Wall* showcases her talents.

Deb Tomaselli

Laura by Vera Caspary (1943)

Like, I suspect, many readers, I came to *Laura* after having reveled a few dozen times in Otto Preminger's shimmering, slinky, near-perfect motion picture, wondering how the book would stack up against that bewitching delight. I was soon floored by the realization that Vera Caspary's novel is deeper, darker, more devious and much, much more disturbing than the movie.

You know the story: Manhattan, early 1940s. "Career girl" Laura Hunt, a successful, single advertising executive, is killed by a disfiguring shotgun blast just before her marriage to a feckless hunk. Investigating is Mark McPherson, a deceptively sensitive blue collar police detective who learns of Laura through the recollections of her intimates, notably Waldo Lydecker, an outsized and outrageous newspaper columnist and professional celebrity who was Laura's self-professed mentor and patron.

The more McPherson absorbs about Laura, the more enamored he becomes of her, but before he is consumed by his love for a woman he could never meet in the flesh, truth literally walks in the door. It upends the case and the lives of all involved, throwing the three men in Laura's life into competition for her body and soul, and compelling all the book's major characters to reassess the differences between covetousness and love, relationships and romantic illusion.

Caspary's masterstroke is splitting her narration among her major characters; each section reflects its narrator's prejudices and perspective, and each speaker conceals — something. This allows Caspary to play with the reader, rearranging time and revelations, withholding and displacing information for maximum effect, permeating each section with ambiguity, generating doubt as to whether what's being professed is the truth, a lie, or what the narrator desperately wants to believe is the truth. As one puts it: "In writing this section ...I have tried to tell what happened as it happened, without too much of my own opinion or prejudice. But I am human."

Caspary's approach is not only an effective technical tool for planting clues and constructing the whodunit puzzle, it's also the fuel that propels the novel to another level, making it not just a wonderful mystery and atmospheric romance but a fascinating, top-notch psychological thriller focused on the vagaries and varieties of human weakness and the strength of character sometimes necessary to just grow up. It also does something the movie does not: it gives Laura Hunt a voice. Far from being the anonymous vessel of men's expectations, she is presented as intelligent, ambitious and accomplished, but bedeviled by doubt and society's expectations of women. And she is also, yes, a bit enigmatic. There are mysteries to Laura. And each reading of the book suggests more of them.

Caspary, who worked her way up in advertising and publishing in Manhattan before turning to writing full time, knew her turf as a worker and a working woman; she also knew people in all their contradictory facets; most important, she knew how to tell one hell of a story. In its themes and tones, its focus on jealousy and possessiveness, on how men view women, and in the depth and complexity of its characters, *Laura* is as immediate and relevant as when it was written 60 years ago. Like the portrait of Laura Hunt which entices Mark McPherson, *Laura* is timeless, haunting and unforgettable.

Ted Fitzgerald

According to the Evidence by Henry Cecil (1954)

A county court judge, Henry Cecil (1902-1976) was a meticulous observer of human nature; his novels revolving around the law are guaranteed to make you laugh out loud at the absurdities of human beings. He is a master of bizarre plot twists and law that boomerangs.

In *According to the Evidence*, Gilbert Essex is tried and acquitted of murdering a young woman he has just met and taken for a short walk. Although the evidence is scant, there is little doubt among those-in-the-know — his lawyer Duffield among others — that he is guilty of at least three murders. At a party immediately after the jurors return their decision, Duffield laments winning the case; a guest hopes for better evidence next time. This casual remark about the probability of a next time troubles Alec Morland, an unmarried artist of independent means. When Essex kills again, twice, someone decides to take matters into their own hands.

At this point, the novel could become a conventional whodunit, with the reader following the investigation of a police detective, a private inquiry agent, or even a zealous amateur. Instead, Cecil focuses on how clever and too-clever-by-half citizens try to manipulate the law, with hilarious and frightening results.

Morland falls in love with Jill Whitby, and in a fit of gentlemanly conscience confesses to Essex's murder. She loves him anyway, but, alas, she's a bit unnerved. To put her mind at rest, she visits Ambrose Low, a reformed criminal now married to a judge's daughter, whose father Low saved from wrongful conviction. Not willing to admit Morland's guilt, but wanting an escape from the nagging possibility of a future marred by a murder conviction, she seeks Low's help. The conversation dances around what could be done, though, of course, since Morland didn't do it, there's no real need to do anything. So begins Low's efforts to have Morland tried, and found not guilty of murder. The evidence implicating Morland appears to be entirely circumstantial, and since no one — including the police — really wants to convict the man who removed the diabolical Essex from the scene, Low's task looks pretty easy. Piece of cake.

Low's plan goes awry several times and he even finds himself in jail for contempt of court. In the end, his plan does not work. It is the perversity of human nature that saves Alec Morland from the gallows.

Cecil is often compared to P.G. Wodehouse, but that comparison only partly explains Cecil's gifts. Yes, he is witty and hilarious, but he also displays a deeper understanding of the devastating misapprehensions of honest people and the miracle that is a functioning legal system. All his books are standalones and are based on his knowledge of the legal system and his experience of human nature. Equally amazing for its wit, humor, and court trial is *Independent Witness* (1963), about a car accident.

Susan Oleksiw

Shadow Of A Broken Man by George C. Chesbro (1977)

If you crave unusual detective fiction, here is your answer. This book provides a unique hardboiled style, with international repercussions, paranormal forays and nifty twists.

I love the way George Chesbro effortlessly blends the outrageous characteristics of his protagonist (reminiscent of suggestions pulled from a hat during some peculiar game) and the book's unlikely premise, and fashions them into a coherent whole. He writes so skillfully, I bought the whole concept. Strange as this case gets — and it *does* get strange — it doesn't require much suspension of disbelief. The action is nonstop, the story is seamless and our hero's qualifications are not gratuitous.

Dr. Robert "Mongo" Frederickson has a private investigator's license, a black belt in karate, a genius IQ and a Ph.D. in criminology, and he teaches at a university. The former circus acrobat/headliner "Mongo the Magnificent" donated time to the United Nations, earning both interesting connections and highly-placed friends. Renaissance man and overachiever, Mongo is a dwarf. He tends to attract the "odd" cases.

Far from being a caricature, Mongo is real, warm and

human, someone we'd want as a friend. As a detective, his grit, intelligence and determination make him exceptional. He's tough but insightful, knowing himself and his limitations. He laughs when it's funny, bleeds when he's cut, cries when he's tortured and keeps on going. He's humble enough to accept help gladly from his NYPD policeman brother, Garth.

For over twenty years, Mongo has remained one of my favorite protagonists, solving memorable crimes involving the paranormal and occult. *Shadow of a Broken Man* is first in the series starring Mongo Frederickson.

The saga begins as Mongo is asked to find a man five years dead. Renowned architect Victor Rafferty had suffered a grievous head injury. Saved by "miracle" surgery, somehow his brain seemed enhanced, rather than diminished. Victor's wounds healed, but he plummeted from a catwalk into a smelting furnace shortly thereafter. The death seemed incontrovertible. Now, Rafferty's widow sees indications he may be alive. Her new husband, former Rafferty contractor Mike Foster, is worried enough to beg Mongo to discreetly investigate the matter. Reluctantly, Mongo accedes to Foster's plea.

Skeptical at first, Mongo unearths odd evidence. Rafferty's surgeon had been killed a mere two days before Rafferty's death, but the case was buried and left unsolved. His search is yielding strange fruit; and now foreign agents and assassins are seeking Rafferty. What can they be after, and why the frenzy and fear? Even if Rafferty were alive, what could an architect know that would compromise international security?

Mary Ann McDonald

Running Blind by Lee Child (2000)

It occurs to me while writing this that readers will wonder why Lee Child is included in this book, given his status. I was astonished to learn he wasn't included in the IMBA *100 Favorite Mysteries of the Century*, and wanted to make sure he was recognized. Fans awarded his first book, *Killing Floor*, the Anthony and Barry Awards for Best First Novel. *Running Blind* was my favorite book of 2000.

Child writes books that can be described in various ways: mysteries, suspense, thrillers and just plain exciting reads. His protagonist is Jack Reacher, a loner and drifter. He had been a military policeman, but is now traveling the United States. He doesn't look for trouble, but neither does he run from a fight.

Reacher is physically a big man, truly deserving of a white hat. Larger than life is an apt description of him. A reluctant hero, one who will help those who need it most, is another description of Reacher. In the series, we see Reacher initially as a drifter who tentatively puts down roots, only to reject that lifestyle. He feels anchored by owning property.

In *Running Blind*, Reacher is the victim of criminal profiling. Several women have been murdered and the common denominator is Reacher. The women had served in the US Army, been harassed, filed complaints, and eventually left the army. The women had few mutual acquaintances, and Reacher was one of them.

The FBI theorizes the killer is a smart guy, a loner, Army, knew the victims, movements unaccounted for, a brutal vigilante personality. The FBI believes that Reacher fits the description. Reacher is forced to investigate the murders to clear his name.

The most effective part of Child's writing is his subtlety. He doesn't bombard the reader with explicit, gratuitous violence and sex, although the books are certainly not cozy. The pacing of the stories is also done to great effect. In *Running Blind*, the majority of the story is told from Reacher's point of view, with occasional scenes from the killers' viewpoint. Toward the end of the book, as the action intensifies, the killers' scenes become more frequent, making the book very exciting.

While it may be necessary to suspend disbelief while reading about Reacher, I do so willingly. Every time I read a Child novel, I am totally drawn into Reacher's world. The action is intense when needed, with well-drawn characters. The settings are a realistic panorama of America and life herein. Reacher is a character I may never run into in real life, so I am glad to read about him.

I look at Reacher as a friend I have not yet had the pleasure to meet in person. I look forward to reading Child over and over as time goes by. If you are a collector of mystery fiction, I feel Reacher is a "must have." If you are a reader, the series will give your reading a jolt of energy.

Maggie Mason

A Famine of Horses by P.F. Chisholm (1994)

I continue to marvel that readers haven't stampeded to a fine four-book (as of 2001) series by P.F. Chisholm, *nom-de-plume* of Britain's Patricia Finney. This series has everything one could want: carefully crafted, clever, challenging plots, a great setting in the border country between England and Scotland, and characters drawn from (Elizabethan) life or wholly from Finney's imagination. And it all begins with horse rustling.

Chisholm has a dazzling ability to plunge her readers straight into the late sixteenth century, straight into the Debatable Lands, the most dangerous part of Elizabeth's kingdom, that border country so porous that blood relations took arms against each other and posses rode back and forth on legitimate hot trods and illegitimate raids. So well transported are we that any interruption becomes unwelcome and we must follow the twists and turns of the plots to the end.

We are led by Sir Robert Carey, the Queen's Deputy Warden, who is stationed in Carlisle. Son of Lord Hunsdon, reputedly Elizabeth's half-brother, Carey, a dandy with expensive tastes and limited income, is a real historical character whose life was itself the stuff of fiction. He's a natural to be the hero of a book, or books, that flesh out the bones of the historical record and embrace not only what we actually know of Carey, but imagine what could have been the truth of his life and character.

Elizabeth Widdrington, too, is a real woman and it's especially to Chisholm's credit that she gives us Elizabeth's character and behavior in a manner consistent with her time and not as rendered through the lens of today's sensibility. The rocky course of the Carey/Widdrington romance is, of course, the very stuff of good fiction.

Other historical personages appear, but the real joy lies less in the real-life figures than in the glorious secondary characters, a ruthless, charming and complex bunch of survivors of what Chisholm spares no pains to reveal as a harsh, unforgiving life. From stalwart Sergeant Dodd to the randy servant Barnabus, you meet them and you know them, just as you learn to wander familiarly among the Grahams and the other Border clans. You could as easily be in our American Wild West, caught up in Tombstone territory.

I write in my introduction to *A Surfeit of Horses*, book three, that what makes me a True Fan — noted by Sharon Kay Penman in hers to *A Famine of Horses*, Dana Stabenow in book two, *A Season of Knives*, and Diana Gabaldon in book four, *A Plague of Angels* — is the language. It is through her lively dialog and unfailingly canny sense of the Right Word that Chisholm conveys the rags and riches of the period and the ins and outs of character. There is no question her research has been prodigious, though it is never flaunted nor allowed to take over the narrative. But somehow, perhaps as a consequence, she has simply stepped into a pattern of speech as into a time warp and sucked us right along with her. It is the web of language she weaves that holds us, once transported to Carey's world, and leaves us reluctant to travel back when the end of the tale is reached. Now we must hope for a fifth: *A Quarrel of Lawyers*.

Barbara Peters

Bucket Nut by Liza Cody (1992)

Eva Wylie is big and tough and touchy; she knows she's uneducated, but she doesn't like to be thought stupid. The truth is that what smarts she has are of the street kind, and she's profoundly ignorant of many of the things the middle class takes for granted. She's also a bagman for a gangster and a semi-pro wrestler, fighting as the London Lassassin. All this makes her an offbeat choice for narrator of a book whose audience is that self-same middle class. Eva's experience and ours overlap only at the outermost edges; she's baffled by things that seem ordinary to us, like antiques ("you'd think that a bloke who could afford a house to himself could afford new furniture. Everything looked really old. I'd bet my Ma's sofa was newer than his, and hers was second-hand"), while hotwiring cars and throwing muscular women around a ring are second nature to her.

The wrestling matches are fantastic. The book opens with one and climaxes with another, each narrated in gritty detail by Eva:

The Blonde Bombshell grabbed a handful of hair and pulled my head up off the canvas. She is such a wanker.

"Watchit," I said. "Mind me teeth."

She knew I had the toothache. But she bashed my face into the floor. Silly cow.

I heaved myself up onto hands and knees with her on my back. She got an arm around my throat. She always gets it wrong: a sort of pinch rather than a lock. But they can't see that even in the front row. And they were really going crazy in the front row.

"Ow-ow-ow," I wailed to encourage them.

...I got the old quads bunched and then slowly I rose to my feet. She was clinging on... She thought I was going to stand upright. She never learns.

Halfway up I went over in a forward roll and dumped her on her back. I twisted and at the last second crashed down on her shoulders. She was too winded to make a bridge. I had her.

The upward arc of Eva's wrestling career is mirrored by the downward arc of the rest of her life when her erstwhile employer decides she must be working for his rivals (she isn't) and tries to blow her up. It turns out that a few things that were obvious to almost everyone concerned — such as the wisdom of avoiding even the appearance of working for two rival gang lords at once — were not obvious to Eva. The climactic wrestling match, in a nice piece of symmetry, pits Eva against a worthy opponent in the ring while the rival gangs beat the hell out of each other at the back of the auditorium.

Liza Cody is the author of two additional Eva Wylie novels, *Monkey Wrench* and *Musclebound,* which are lively and engaging stories despite the continuing downward trajectory of Eva's luck. (Though it must be said that *Musclebound* stops, frustratingly, without coming to an end — it's hard to recall another book that leaves so many loose ends.) Cody also writes a series about Anna Lee, a London PI whose peripheral role in *Bucket Nut* will amuse readers of the Anna Lee books. The Anna Lee series begins with *Dupe*.

Beth Thoenen

Without Lawful Authority by Manning Coles (1943)

Soothing spy story is an unlikely phrase, but an apt descriptor for a Manning Coles mystery. Adelaide Frances Oke Manning (1891-1959) and Cyril Henry Coles (1899-1965) were an unlikely pair. Her biography is sparse: she attended a girls' high school; during World War I she worked in a munitions factory and at the War Office. After army service and work with British Intelligence in World War I, he was a railway worker, garage manager and newspaper columnist in Australia; he married after returning to England; there were two sons. He served again with British Intelligence during World War II. He had adventures, and she did not, but they ended up as neighbors in a small Hampshire town, and between 1940 and 1963, as "Manning Coles," they published 24 books — now out of print and out of fashion. No sex: a gentle love story as a sideline. No contrived horror: history of the time is worse than any imaginings. No ambiguity: we aren't invited to observe that good is fraught with evil, and evil quite excusable. No strictures against laughing at what now must be taken seriously. But, if you'll risk all that, search the shelves in dusty bookshops. My copy of *Without Lawful Authority* is a dingy, stained hardback, its endpaper inscribed "Library of Rose Berkowitz Glens Falls, N.Y." The facing page gives the sale price ($2.00), and a pre-title page notes, "This is Manning Coles' longest book. In wartime conservation of paper the book has been set with a longer line."

Coles' series protagonist is Thomas Elphinstone Hambledon, whose early career as a headmaster is occasionally useful: *"If I were you, Palmer, I'd try and be civil; that is, if you know how. I dislike impertinence, Palmer."* Once, suffering from amnesia, he rose to an important position under Hitler; having recovered his senses he supplied information to the British. As this story opens, he is, unobtrusively, a power in the Foreign Office; we find him, in mid-story, chafing at "having to be so infernally law-abiding." Since law-abidingness is not one of the charms of the series, the book opens with another protagonist. A young man named Warnford lives, idle and isolated, with Ashling, his devoted servant; one fortunate night his flat is burgled by a fellow named Marden. Warnford was court-martialed after important papers in his safe went missing; a tutorial in burglary may help him discover how he was framed.

Thus begin the trio's picaresque adventures, recounted in chapters with such titles as "Dark Deeds in Kent" and "Pork and Diamonds." What fun the authors must have had, plotting together, and swapping ideas for dialog — *"Discretion,"* *repeated Hambledon urgently. "My dear sir,"* [says a hotel manager] *"discretion has become the envelope of my immortal soul"* — and topping up with their signature feature, the lunatic asylum episode. Here a German spy — the very one who framed Warnford—controls the asylum. Warnford and Marden are held captive; Hambledon has climbed over the wall disguised as St. Francis of Assisi, and unlocked the wrong set of doors, releasing, among others, a soi-disant Benvenuto Cellini and a Louis XVI. *A little fat man emerged. He took in the situation at a glance, said, "the official attendants instantly released must emphatically be," and bolted upstairs.*

How soothing!

Jeanne M. Jacobson

The Man in the Green Chevy by Susan Rogers Cooper (1988)

I recently reread *The Man in the Green Chevy* and my first thought was — how great to sit down with an old friend like Milt Kovak again. Milt is funny, self-deprecating and easy to be with, but a real man too. Susan Cooper received letters from men swearing she had to be a man using a female pseudonym because Milt rings true.

Chief Deputy Kovak is head of the homicide unit of Prophesy County, Oklahoma, which is laughable since the aforementioned unit consists of Milt and anybody else he can shanghai to help. Milt got the title when Barnie Littlefield shot his wife and Milt found Barnie standing over his wife's body saying "That's the last time I'm eating her meatloaf." Solving that case and keeping his dinner down at the scene of a big wreck on Interstate 12 brought him his fancy title. It also cost him his marriage. Maybe the fact that he often tuned her out had something to do with her leaving. She was gone two days before he missed her.

In this, Milt Kovak's first big case, a rapist and murderer is on the loose in Prophesy County and his victims are elderly women. Milt wonders what the world is coming to. Milt talks to his prime witness, who's just about the sexiest woman he's ever seen. He's dismayed to learn Laura is married and the mother of three children but that fact doesn't keep him from lusting after her and her after him. Laura describes a 1970s model green Chevrolet Impala with a male driver about 30 years old on the victim's street.

I always know when I pick up a Milt Kovak mystery that I will be entertained, I'll laugh a little, maybe cry a little but I will thoroughly enjoy myself. How Milt came about is quite a tale. Susan tells of how her husband, Don, wanted her to write this novel he had plotted, a spy/adventure/mystery/thriller about a guy running through the woods with a beautiful babe on one arm and a gun on the other arm. Susan tried writing Don's story but a guy named Milt kept intruding. She secretly began writing the Milt story — having an affair with Milt Kovak every afternoon — and when she was halfway through the book, she finally showed it to Don. He liked it and told her to go ahead and write the Milt story. The rest, as they say, is history.

Susan has written two other series, one featuring stand-up comedienne Kimmey Kruse and, more recently, the Edgar-nominated, highly acclaimed E.J. Pugh series. Unfortunately, we all know how those honors and acclaims don't always translate into bigger sales. We sold many copies of Susan's books in our store but for the last few years as we sold the E.J. Pugh series, we were asked routinely "When is Susan doing a new Milt?" I finally have a positive answer and also have the honor of being one of the first to announce that Susan is writing a new Milt, titled *Lying Wonders*, which St. Martin's will publish in 2002. The beautiful, sexy Laura from *The Man in the Green Chevy* is back in town and Milt, the happily-married new father, is facing all sorts of new problems.

Jan Grape

A Show of Hands by David A. Crossman (1997)

Although *A Show of Hands* is sometimes sad and occasionally unsettling, it is at heart a "feel good" book — gentle, wise, witty and, well, just plain sweet. I don't much enjoy reading about sadistic serial killers or graphic violence, and I prefer mysteries that are more thoughtful and realistic than a lot of today's cozies. This literate, engrossing, endearing book fits the bill on both counts.

The hero is not a perky amateur sleuth, a wisecracking PI or a battle-scarred cop, but an elderly retiree returned to the quiet Maine island where he grew up. Winston Crisp is distinguished from the other old salts with whom he sits and gossips around the stove at the hardware store largely by a more enquiring and logical mind, honed through a lifetime "away," working as the NSA's chief code breaker. Despite his colorful career, he looks forward to the uneventful twilight of his life, as both his mental and physical powers start to fade. But the odd circumstances of a local murder — and the victim's ghostly, half-felt presence — rally him to try to find the evil mind behind the killing. Assisted by the amiable island policeman, a perspicacious investigator from the mainland, and a fiery young "big city" attorney, Winston slowly picks his way through the contradictory and confusing elements of the case towards a dangerous denouement.

This story swims in vivid local color, with the salty characters around the hardware store stove serving as a kind of offbeat Greek chorus, while the sea breezes whistle and whisper across the pages. David Crossman's characters are eccentric originals who make themselves comfortable in the corners of our minds. His prose is enriched by a poet's cadence, a pitch-perfect ear for the down-east drawl, and a light and easy grace that makes metaphor feel right at home. Here's the scene at the stove shortly after the body of the murder victim, Amanda Murphy, has been discovered:

An old ship's clock on the wall opposite the men had the Millberry's Magnesia logo etched in ornate frosted letters on its glass case. It kept perfect time — seven minutes slow. Always had been. On the island, "I'll be there 'bout Millberry time" meant a little late. During lapses in conversation old eyes often settled on the pendulum in a ritual of self hypnosis. It was the only thing that moved, gently knocking the seconds aside like dominos.

Crisp was having a hard time concentrating. He couldn't get Amanda Murphy out of his mind. He never saw her face directly, only in reflections — in windows as she stopped for a moment to peer out into the stark sunlight, or in smoky mirrors as she passed by. Room to room. Slowly. Silently. Room to room. Ticktock, ticktock.

Crossman's first book, *Murder in a Minor Key*, was a knockout laugh-out-loud (and cry-yourself-to-sleep) standalone. Way too many years passed before *Show of Hands* appeared, happily followed by a sequel in fairly short order. Fans of the elegant and the offbeat can only hope a fourth title is on the way soon.

Jill Hinckley

Rough Cut by Stan Cutler (1994)

Stan Cutler's novels set in Hollywood are a very funny series that combines social satire with mystery. Cutler does a masterful job of creating two separate and very distinct voices — Rayford Goodman, PI to the Stars, a Philip Marlowe type who is somewhat out of his element in 1990s Southern California, and Mark Bradley, a thirtysomething gay writer who is very much *in* his element in 1990s Southern California. Their collaboration in writing Hollywood true crime books becomes a collaboration in solving mysteries as well. The odd-couple pairing never becomes cutesy, because Cutler is so true to the two voices.

More important even than the characters, this is a mystery series where the setting is the key to understanding both the main characters and the crimes they investigate. Neither the sleuths nor the crimes could occur, say, in Iowa. In the first of the series, award-winning *Best Performance by a Patsy*, the two join forces to write about a murder from Hollywood's Golden Age, and end up finding the real killer.

The murder that they investigate in *Rough Cut* is that of an over-the-hill starlet, famous for baring her breasts at Hollywood galas, and now making ends meet with some casual hooking. The cast of suspects is very Southern California — a sleazy producer, an unsavory director of porn movies, a drug-dealer, an over-the-hill actress turned businesswoman and a mysterious politician. The motives for the murder quickly become apparent and are tied in to Hollywood's second most lucrative industry after moviemaking — real estate.

Rough Cut exemplifies the strength of the series as it hearkens back to the Golden Age of Hollywood — the dog who finds the starlet's missing diary is, naturally, named Asta — while it examines completely contemporary themes of greed, power and dirty politics. In *The Face on the Cutting Room Floor,* Mark and Ray investigate the mob-related murder of an Oscar-winning film director. In *Shot on Location*, they exonerate a famous actor accused of shooting his sister's lover and his father.

Cutler is a master at giving stereotypical Hollywood types and situations a fresh and insightful spin. He undercuts the reader's assumptions at every turn, beginning with his main characters. Ray is never as much of a Neanderthal as he appears and Mark is never as much the shallow yuppie. Both men are essentially decent and respect each other despite their differences. It's interesting that when their researcher is the victim of date rape, both men agree — only partly hyperbolically — that the just thing to do is kill the rapist. Ultimately, Ray and Mark are both outsiders in Hollywood society and it is this perspective that makes them such wonderful observers of the narcissistic excesses of a totally self-absorbed society. It is Cutler's ability to combine social satire with brilliant mystery characterization and plotting that elevates this series above the norm.

Christine Acevedo

Murders in Volume 2 by Elizabeth Daly (1941)

She was said to be Dame Agatha Christie's favorite writer of detective stories, and she didn't begin her brief career as a mystery writer until she was 62, when her first novel, *Unexpected Night*, was published. This book introduced the bibliophile detective, Henry Gamadge, to the world. With his wide range of bibliographic skills, Gamadge often found himself involved in cases requiring the kinds of arcane knowledge which seemingly only he possessed. With his rumpled suits and upper-crust New York upbringing, he moved in the highest circles of Murray Hill society, not unlike his transatlantic counterpart, Lord Peter Wimsey. The late, great Anthony Boucher once wrote that Gamadge was so well bred, however, as to make even Lord Peter seem a trifle coarse! Gamadge has a cat named Martin and an assistant named Harold Bantz, and in the third novel in the series, *Murders in Volume 2*, he meets a young woman, Clara Dawson, who becomes his wife.

All of Elizabeth Daly's sixteen Gamadge novels contain the classic elements of Golden Age detective fiction — enclosed, often isolated, settings, obscure clues and a small circle of closely connected suspects. Daly also had a fondness for spooky elements, as in *Murders in Volume 2*, in which a young woman claims to be the reincarnation of a missing nineteenth-century governess. The reappearance of a missing volume of Byron's poetry in the Vauregard mansion is a key clue in the case, and it is this that brings Gamadge into the picture. He finds in the Vauregard family a stifling atmosphere, in which propriety must be observed and preserved at all costs. That murder should dare intrude into such hallowed halls is the ultimate insult. But murder does shatter the desiccated peace of the Vauregards, and Gamadge has to catch the murderer and protect Clara Dawson from danger.

Daly, like her admirer Agatha Christie, had a knack for finding the sinister in the ordinary, domestic details of life, and her elegantly constructed novels are some of the most delightfully satisfying examples of late Golden Age detective fiction. Daly is my favorite American writer from this period because I find her characters so attractive and so much more real than those of S.S. Van Dine and Ellery Queen, to cite the two most famous American detective-story writers of the era. While the Philo Vance and Ellery Queen stories now seem much more arid and more highly artificial, the Gamadge novels retain a charm and a liveliness that makes them still eminently readable. Daly, like her peers, took pains to create fair puzzles, and readers who like to match wits with a clever sleuth can have a lot of fun with Henry Gamadge. Daly herself thought that the detective story was an important literary form, and her mysteries shine as beautiful examples of the genre.

Dean James

Good Cop, Bad Cop by Barbara D'Amato (1998)

I was going to write a nice neat little essay about *Good Cop, Bad Cop*, and I even had one started, but then I started to think about what it was that drew me to this series in the first place. Jeanne Dams had been in our bookstore signing copies of her latest book when we got to talking about Barbara D'Amato, a friend of Jeanne's. She said *Killer.app* had kept her up all night long and went on to rave about it. Because I had enjoyed the Cat Marsala books, and trusting Jeanne's judgment (impeccable),

I picked up *Killer.app* myself. After that I was on a total D'Amato jag — I read all of the series published at the time and now breathlessly await the latest one each time it appears. *Good Cop, Bad Cop* happens to be my favorite so far because I'm a fan of the neat structure, but you can't go wrong reading any of this series about a group of Chicago cops.

This series comes mid-career for D'Amato; having established herself as a competent, entertaining writer of fairly standard PI novels featuring investigative journalist Cat Marsala, something pushed her ahead to a higher plateau. A lot of the things that were so terrific about her Cat Marsala books — her firm grounding in her Chicago setting, her skillful use of research integrated into the plots, and most of all her ability to write a suspenseful scene that has you on the edge of your seat as much as any movie ever did or will — are put to use in this series, but here they are perfectly blended. Each book focuses on slightly different characters, but beat cop Suze Figueroa appears in all of them, and is more or less the main character. In *Good Cop, Bad Cop* the focus is slightly different — it's on "bad" cop Aldo Bertolucci, and "good" cop, Nick Bertolucci, Aldo's brother, who is not only a cop but the superintendent of police.

There are lots of opposites and comparisons in this book, with the two brothers being the most obvious — why have they turned out so differently, though they've grown up in exactly the same environment? This is probably the central question of the novel. Aldo blows every chance he gets; Nick makes the most of his opportunities and ends up superintendent. Aldo and his partner are also a study in contrasts — Aldo is old, fat and cranky; his partner, the unfortunate Dick-dick, is young, enthusiastic and energetic. Suze stands out from practically all the other cops simply because she's a woman. There's also the contrast between Nick and his deputy, Gus. Nick is white, Gus is black; Nick is an outgoing pol, Gus stays in the background. The racial gulf between them is even addressed in a heartbreaking speech toward the end of the book.

But beyond the neat structure, this book also presents a well-written, compelling, deftly told story. The combination makes for an enjoyable book that can keep you up all night.

Robin Agnew

The Victim in Victoria Station by Jeanne M. Dams (1999)

Returning to a favorite book is somewhat like sitting down to visit with old friends. Whether it's a Lori Shepherd, a Mrs. Pollifax or a Dorothy Martin one pulls down from the shelf, getting involved with the characters once again provides a much needed respite from real life and its trials. Sometimes just reading about these Americans and their adventures abroad lends a healthy dose of escapism to ease one through the day. All three enlist the aid of strangers they've befriended to accomplish great tasks and to bring criminals to justice. They instill hope that a brighter tomorrow really does exist.

Such a tale is *The Victim in Victoria Station*, fifth in the series and one of my personal favorites. Here we find Dorothy Martin, frazzled and late for her doctor's appointment, discovering a dead man on the train. Lucky for her, another doctor comes along to offer to summon authorities, preventing any further delay for Dorothy's orthopedist's appointment. Only later does Dorothy start to wonder why the man's death was never recorded in the newspapers, the police logs or anywhere. Who was this mysterious stranger and what became of him? How will she ever find out?

Jeanne M. Dams draws Dorothy Martin as an older woman, now married to a retired British police officer. It's Dorothy's soothing voice telling the tale. Her love of England and her penchant for colorful chapeaux make her a sympathetic protagonist who must deal with physical frailties this time out, too. Dorothy's quest is further complicated by her lack of knowledge about and experience with computers. Never fear, she's soon won over to word processing, which she thinks of as typing without the whiteout and the erasures.

Computers figure prominently in the plot, too, and readers soon discover that ignorance of their workings is no hardship for a persistent sleuth like Dorothy. She's soon involved with software pirating and goes undercover at the London office of an international software developer. A friend's hacking into the company's employee roster points the way to numerous motives.

Dams displays numerous gifts in the telling of this tale. She offers crisp dialog that not only defines the character but moves the plot forward too. Dorothy's voice has a rhythm that begs reading aloud. It makes Dorothy's love of England evident in every utterance. Dams makes the English rain real in the way she describes Dorothy's experiences with it. Dams shows a keen eye and ear for human interaction and conflict, too. She knows how to show someone falling to pieces and she knows how to show someone hiding behind lies and subterfuge. She explores our feelings about old age and physical limitation.

Dams celebrates old age by showing us that growing older doesn't have to mean a loss of mental acuity and productivity. Her cheerful optimism permeates every page of this charming English cozy.

I know this is one book I'll read again.

Geraldine Galentree

Irene's Last Waltz by Carole Nelson Douglas (1994) aka Another Scandal in Bohemia

When the versatile Carole Nelson Douglas turned her genre-tweaking skills toward mystery, she filled a gap on the Sherlockian shelf by amending Doyle's account of Irene Adler in "A Scandal in Bohemia." With *Good Night, Mr. Holmes*

(1990), Douglas ushered in a 1990s explosion of women-centered history-mystery reschooling us about the ornery presence of women in both social and literary history.

So what really happened in "A Scandal in Bohemia"? According to Watson, Sherlock Holmes is smitten by the only woman Doyle ever allowed to outfox him, an adventuress of "dubious and questionable memory." Irene Adler, romantically linked to the King of Bohemia, is an American diva possessing a photograph the king claims could compromise his political marriage and upset European stability. But by the end of the king's case, Irene Adler has become for Sherlock Holmes "THE woman" above all others.

Shifting her flamboyant but principled Irene Adler from the margin to the center of the Bohemian narrative, Douglas somehow remains true to Doyle's Holmes at the same time she elaborates his relation to a woman as extraordinary as himself. Using signature flair and derring-do, Irene Adler has by the end of *Good Night, Mr. Holmes* extricated herself from crimes personal and the king from crimes political. By the by, she establishes herself as Holmes's formidable mirror image: married woman, professional musician and occasional sleuth.

Repeatedly throughout her hundred-year history, Irene Adler has survived the convenient death Doyle invented for her, and now she is about to be resurrected from publishing's backlist. In 2001, after a seven-year lapse, Irene's fifth adventure *Chapel Noir* appeared, to be followed in 2002 by the sixth, *Castle Rouge*. Early in 2003, the fourth novel, *Irene's Last Waltz* will be republished as *Another Scandal in Bohemia*, followed by series starter *Good Night, Mr. Holmes*; *Good Morning, Irene* (1991) as *The Adventuress*; and *Irene At Large* (1992) as *A Soul of Steel*.

As its new name ("another scandal") indicates, *Irene's Last Waltz* revisits Prague, where this time something is even more rotten in the state of Bohemia. Irene's former suitor has mysteriously failed to consummate his political marriage to a

45

Scandinavian princess, and he flaunts his Russian mistress before a kingdom fissured by political nationalism and economic stress. Rumor even reports that Rabbi Loew's ancient clay Golem stalks the streets, serving Jews notice to beware chaos.

Perilous dueling in Prague's royal court is between women, even though Sherlock Holmes has also been summoned into this case linking fashion and the foreign office. But Holmes, who still has a lot to learn about female worlds, can only admire Irene's remarkable resolution of international crises from the sidelines. Fearless, Irene takes a hint from *The Prisoner of Zenda* and rebounds Russian spy and femme fatale Tatyana's deadly craft against her.

Retitling and repackaging Irene's early escapades may well rescue her for the truly broad audience she should have had from the first. Neither the title *Irene's Last Waltz* nor its jacket (featuring attractive dancers gazing into each other's eyes) suggest the prodigal intrigue and literary buffoonery actually found inside. As *Another Scandal in Bohemia*, the book's high-concept hijinks and zealous purpose will better bridge the series' swashbuckling beginnings to *Chapel Noir*'s graver turn in a nineteenth century progressing toward catastrophe.

Jo Ellyn Clarey

Matricide at St. Martha's by Ruth Dudley Edwards (1994)

If the question is, "Is nothing sacred?", the answer is — resoundingly — "No!" Ruth Dudley Edwards' Robert Amiss crime fiction series is some of the best satire you'll ever read. My all time favorite is *Matricide at St. Martha's*, probably because this book introduces the redoubtable Baroness Jack Troutbeck (who isn't yet a baroness — that comes two books later). In *Matricide*, Amiss has accepted a one-year fellowship at St. Martha's College, Cambridge, just as the school is riven with academic/political rivalries that erupt in murder (by defenestration). The rival factions — and there are many, including bluestockings, sybarites and the politically correct brigade — at this least well known of the Cambridge colleges that has been "staggering along on a shoestring in an undistinguished sort of way for 80 years or so" all believe they deserve the lion's share of a benefactor's largesse and someone has gone to murderous lengths to get the ten million quid.

Who can resist a book that begins:

"Balls!" said the Bursar and continued skipping vigorously. As her skirt rode higher, vast quantities of satin eau-de-Nil directoire knicker were exposed to Amiss's enchanted gaze.

"Sod This!" she shouted a couple of minutes later. Flinging the skipping-rope into the corner of her office, she marched back to the desk, threw herself into her chair and lit one of the pipes that peeped out from under the litter of papers.

Edwards is a noted historian, journalist, biographer, political critic and essayist, and novelist. In addition to her own works of history, biography and fiction, Edwards has published numerous book reviews on history, current affairs and fiction in English and Irish newspapers and journals over the last thirty years. Other titles in the Robert Amiss series include *Corridors of Death, The St. Valentine's Day Murders, The English School of Murder, Clubbed to Death, Ten Lords A-Leaping, Murder in a Cathedral, Publish and be Murdered* and *The Anglo-Irish Murders*. Just read them all — you'll be glad you did!

Kathryn Kennison

The Portland Laugher by Earl Emerson (1994)

My lack of visitors continues to baffle me.

Thus we find Seattle PI Thomas Black at the beginning of
The Portland Laugher, hospitalized in a semi-comatose state,
able to hear and think, but not move or communicate. Black is
particularly puzzled by the absence of Kathy Birchfield, his
professional associate, best friend and the woman to whom he
has lately professed his love. Having no recollection of recent
events, Black broods about how he came to be in his present
condition, while the story unfolds for the reader in a series of
flashbacks.

It seems that several months earlier, Black had been asked by
a client to follow Kathy's fiancé, Philip Bacon. He knew that
taking the case was a bad idea — what could be a worse
transgression than tailing the fiancé of the woman you love? —
but he was sure Philip was up to something and he couldn't
resist the opportunity to catch him at it.

The plot of *The Portland Laugher* (a dark story, despite the
title) will keep you turning the pages until the riveting end, but
it's Emerson's prose style that makes him stand out from the
crowd. I love his way with language, his humor and his
characters. Thomas Black and Kathy Birchfield are nice people
that you'd enjoy knowing, even though in this book they aren't
exactly putting their best feet forward. Thomas hilariously
taunts Philip to his face and jeers at him behind his back, while
Kathy's indecision and irrational stand-by-your-man attitude
toward her fiancé seem maddeningly immature. In other words,
they act just as you might expect real people to act in their shoes.

As in all of Emerson's books, the supporting characters are
so vividly portrayed that you'd swear you recognize them.
Consider Black's friend Snake — Elmer Slezak — an ex-cop,
now considered to be Tacoma's sleaziest private investigator,
a character whose many peccadilloes give the author plenty of

opportunity for comic relief:

*Once in my truck, Elmer Slezak sat like a kid, with one leg
and boot up on the bench seat and his spine squared up against
the door so that should it pop open, he would shoot across the
highway like a runaway corpse, a misadventure that had
actually happened to Snake while taking a cab to his father's
funeral, and, because it had happened to the kind of stubborn
man that Snake was, he reacted in the way of stubborn men by
sitting that way pretty much exclusively from then on.*

Or take Philip, an inveterate liar with one blue eye and one
brown, who winks at everyone. Thomas likes to call him "old
blue eye." I'm sure I know this guy. I'll bet you do, too.

With eleven Thomas Black mysteries and five Mac Fontana
books under his belt, as well as a Shamus award and an Edgar
nomination, Earl Emerson, a lieutenant with the Seattle fire
department, is certainly not unknown to mystery fans. He is,
however, underappreciated, especially by neophyte mystery
readers, because several of his books are no longer readily
available.

The Portland Laugher is the seventh in the Thomas Black
series, which began with *The Rainy City* (1985). Black last
appeared in *Catfish Café* (1998). Emerson's other mystery
series features Mac Fontana, a firefighter in Staircase,
Washington. His next book, *Vertical Burn*, a nonseries thriller,
is due in 2002.

Karen Spengler

Jitterbug by Loren D. Estleman (1998)

Although there are many wonderful novels in Loren
Estleman's Detroit series, *Jitterbug* is my absolute favorite.
Each book in this ambitious series is set in a different decade of

its namesake's history, and features recurring characters who age and change as time passes, alongside real figures of the era — in *Jitterbug's* case, a decrepit Henry Ford. As you might guess from the title, it's set in the '40s during the second world war, and covers a lot of ground, featuring two parallel plots that intersect, but only tangentially. One thread involves a serial killer, who, kept out of the army on a section eight, decides to help the war effort by bayoneting ration stamp hoarders and repossessing their stamps for "the boys at the front." The other story involves two black brothers, Earl and Dwight Littlejohn, who move up to Ypsilanti, Michigan from Alabama in order to build airplanes in Henry Ford's Willow Run plant. Although it sounds like a sweeping historical epic, *Jitterbug* is a tight, concise novel, at once a page turner about the pursuit of a serial killer, a thoughtful examination of racism, and a masterful evocation of the experiences of living through a world war. For those of us who've never gotten closer to the war than finding a forgotten book of ration stamps in granny's old cupboard, there are many fascinating insights.

But what really sparkles in *Jitterbug* is the prose, a neglected part of so many modern mysteries whose workmanlike words merely push the plot forward. Estleman fits comfortably in the glorious continuum of American crime fiction stylists like Dashiell Hammett, Raymond Chandler and Ross Macdonald, and his virtuosity is one of the reasons I enjoy his books so much. Here's his description of Dwight Littlejohn's introduction to the downtown police station:

Dwight vaguely remembered hearing that Detroit Police Headquarters was designed by the same man who had laid out the Willow Run plant, but he couldn't see much of a family resemblance between that utilitarian barn and the corridor where he stood waiting for an elevator to come and get him ... even the casual squalor of the police couldn't cloud the Roman Empire authoritarianism of the architect's vision. He was

*aware of the dirt under his nails and the fact that his shoes
needed polishing. He suspected it was part of the plan that he
felt like a flea in a cathedral.*

This passage accomplishes so much — it immediately and
concretely evokes a certain place while at the same time
capturing the character's state of mind within that place, as
Dwight, a single black man in a huge building full of white
policemen, wishes for nothing more than invisibility. *Jitterbug*
is full of such transcendent passages, which may, unfortunately,
explain Estleman's lack of bestseller status — the brain must be
firmly in the "on" position to enjoy his novels. But to the serious
mystery reader this is not a barrier but an inducement, and if
you're in search of a most rewarding reading experience look
no further than Estleman and his great novel *Jitterbug*.

Robin Agnew

Death of the Duchess by Elizabeth Eyre (1992)

Imagine opening a gloriously illuminated fifteenth century
manuscript, whose pages swell miraculously till the landscape
becomes three-dimensional and the figures begin to move and
speak. The Prince has given orders: *the precious box of lapis
lazuli, so carefully listed in his accounts, should be fetched and
some be weighed out.... For the Princess, skies should be
magnificently blue.* Enter and watch the pageants unfold.

Once each year from 1992 to 1997, the authors who wrote as
Elizabeth Eyre offered such a pageant: *Death of the Duchess,
Curtains for the Cardinal, Poison for the Prince, Bravo for the
Bride, Axe for an Abbot, Dirge for a Dog*e. Begin, ideally, at the
beginning. One of many joys of the series is that as Sigismondo
and his servant Benno travel through the principalities of Italy,
they encounter again intriguing people from earlier adventures.
Not all, of course, not the duchess whose death is signaled by

the title, nor the traitor whose villainy has been concealed behind a benign mask — *May all such traitors have such an end* — but the blonde and impetuous daughter of the Duke's favorite mistress; the duke's crippled nephew; a placid widow not averse to sharing her favors with Sigismondo; and an angelically beautiful thief skilled in knife-throwing, dancing, fortune-telling and disguise. In the climactic scene, a crowd awaits the execution of an accused murderer — who at that moment is watching from a balcony with the cheerful widow and the pretty daughter of his family's greatest enemy. Dramatically, the Duke himself is denounced as the true murderer; when the Duchess' brother turns to attack, his sword arm is grasped by the Lady Violante. Their vigorous struggle inspires desire, and Duke Yppolito and the Duchess Violante take center stage in two later tales. The "bravo" of one of the titles may be Sigismondo himself, hired to accompany a petulant bride to her wedding with a man whose sole attraction is his wealth.

The stories are set, in time and place, in the midst of the Renaissance: the time is the fifteenth century, the place is Italy — but they are not typical medieval mysteries. Other novels in that wonderfully entertaining subgenre are historically-based. Fictional characters mingle with real members of the nobility and clergy, with warriors and artists and courtesans whose names can found in accounts of the times. Their plots are set in the midst of battles and plagues and intrigues and religious controversies that we can read about in history books and encyclopedias. The mysteries in this series, in contrast, are like paintings. We see a world complete in itself. And all who enter come as equals — no one is hampered by too little historical knowledge; no one is burdened by too much. Every person and every event is wholly fictitious, and the features of this colorful world are so brilliantly depicted that they remain a vivid part of our mental landscape.

Jeanne M. Jacobson

Kill Me Again by Terence Faherty (1996)

During the war, Scott Elliott tells us, he and his fellow soldiers would imagine themselves doing "perfectly ordinary things" as a coping mechanism, giving how-to talks to each other. Elliott's topic was "Mixing a Gibson." After the fighting, he ended up with five buddies in a bar in Paris where he ...

... mixed five Gibsons, one at a time, with hands that actually trembled. We'd raised them in a toast to nothing in particular or maybe to everything.

The faces of those farm boys had been as alive with light as the cocktails themselves as we'd stood staring at our glasses. Then we'd drunk, and the lights had blinked out, one by one. The magic of the moment had disappeared, trampled by a chorus of orders for beer chasers. The real Gibsons had failed to live up to the expectations created by months of imaginary ones, even for me.

I've never had a Gibson myself, but the writing here is so vivid that it doesn't matter: I know what Gibsons mean to Elliott, and Terence Faherty's description makes it easy to picture that moment of disappointment. He goes on: "It had been a foretaste of my return to civilian life, though I hadn't recognized that nuance at the time. Despite that notable failure, I'd stuck to Gibsons."

There are so many reasons to like *Kill Me Again* that it's hard to know where to start. What jumps out first is the love of movies. Before the war, Elliott was a bit player on the verge of becoming a star. On his return, he found Hollywood uninterested. But he's thoroughly infected with "movie fever," so he doesn't return home to Indiana. Instead, he becomes a private detective, working for the Hollywood Security Agency.

It's 1947, and efforts are underway to film a sequel to *Passage to Lisbon* (read *Casablanca*). The studio receives a worrisome letter: "Why are you using a Communist writer on *Love Me Again?*"

Faherty paints a great portrait of the movie business, and Elliott's fever is contagious. His idea for a *Casablanca* sequel — the names have been changed, but you'll recognize the situation and the characters — is truly wonderful, picking up a thread from the original and twisting it in a way that's clever, appreciative and believable. Even if *Kill Me Again* had no other virtues, this thread would be enough to recommend it — it's great fun.

But there is a lot more going on here. For one thing, Faherty's portrait is of a Hollywood in transition. He touches on the end of the studio system and — as the threatening note indicates — the beginning of the Red Scare. Elliott himself is in transition, returning to real life after his brushes with stardom before the war and mortality during the war. Along with others he encounters, in a case that becomes quite complicated, Elliott has to deal with the problem of "living the rest of your life with the knowledge that you've had your best day."

Finally, the writing is pure pleasure. Elliott plays the role of private detective perfectly, falling for a dame and delivering witty comebacks. The dialog is sharp and funny, just like you'd expect from great '40s films.

Faherty's published two more Scott Elliott novels, *Come Back Dead* (winner of the Shamus Award) and *Raise the Devil*, and he's also the author of the Owen Keane series. I recommend them all.

Jim Huang

Pest Control by Bill Fitzhugh (1997)

The hardboiled crime novel is an important subgenre in the mystery field, and Bill Fitzhugh has offered a highly original and extremely funny addition to it, joining the likes of Carl

Hiassen, Fred Willard and Elmore Leonard.

Bob Dillon, perhaps one of the most likable protagonists in recent years, is an exterminator looking for his place in the world. His dream is to launch his all-natural environmentally-friendly pest elimination technique to the world, and get a fiberglass bug on the roof of his vehicle. When he loses his job for a corporate pest elimination company, Bob places an ad in the classifieds proclaiming his services, which is read by a crime outfit overseas. The "exterminator for hire" is misconstrued and Bob is suddenly hired as an assassin.

When Bob receives several packages through the mail containing many large bills in return for his services, it becomes painfully obvious to everyone but Bob that something is amiss. People are dying and Bob, who participates in their deaths, is getting the credit. This stirs many of the top assassins in the world: Klaus (the world's top hit man), a cowboy, a tall supermodel-sized seductress, a transvestite dwarf and a fashion-addicted Italian. All they want is to reclaim the title of "Best Assassin," the title Bob now holds through no fault of his own. Another group seems to be taking an interest in Bob as well — the CIA. Through the streets of New York, a chase ensues. Bob faces a race against time, bullets and eviction to find out what he's plummeted himself into, as well as who is actually offing people under his name.

Fitzhugh takes us on a wild roller-coaster ride through the dark streets of New York City, brilliantly introducing us to well-drawn characters that seem as far out in left field as a Far Side comic, and throwing around a barrage of witty dialog and clever puns. Fitzhugh also tosses out subtle entomological trivia, adding to the charm of the book. The book's action picks up immediately, and reads as if you are watching a movie. Perhaps this is because Fitzhugh originally wrote this as a screenplay, and transcribed the piece into a novel. My only complaint with the book was that I read it one sitting, and was desperate to find more of his writings.

Although Bill Fitzhugh has never made a bestseller list, nor has he launched a huge global tour, he is the author of three other amusing reads, *The Organ Grinders*, *Cross Dressing* and *Fender Benders*. Fitzhugh was born and raised in Jackson, Mississippi and has written for radio and the Internet, and assisted in writing the script for the "Monty Python and the Holy Grail" CD-ROM game.

Eric Mays

Murder in the OPM by Leslie Ford (1942)

Writing under the pen name Leslie Ford, Zenith Brown created the unforgettable detective team of Mrs. Grace Latham, Col. Primrose and Sgt. Buck. They appeared in many of her mysteries, but *Murder in the OPM* is an especially good example because it takes place in Washington during World War II. The stories are told by Mrs. Latham, a young widow whose children are usually away at school. She lives in Georgetown with her "colored" help Lilac and has a busy schedule of volunteer activities, social events and crime solving in the relatively upper class white strata of year-round Washington society.

The best part of her mysteries is her (often unconsciously telling) sense of time and place. *Murder in the OPM* takes place shortly after the bombing of Pearl Harbor, when people started to pour into Washington to support the war effort. Much to her surprise, the retired Col. Primrose, who lives right around the corner on P Street, and Sgt. Phineas T. Buck do not return to active duty. Instead they stay in Washington and rather mysteriously seem to be involved in investigating crime in some official capacity that is not clear to her or us. While there is some flirtation between Primrose and Latham, fate and Buck seem to conspire to keep it from anything near consummation.

Latham seems to function as Primrose's eyes and ears as she

has entree into homes that are well-insulated from official inquiries of any kind. She is the one who is invited over for tea and finds herself alone with the crying daughter who pours her heart out, or sees the father's fit of temper at the mention of a name. She has a habit of jumping to the conclusion that Primrose is after a person for whom she has developed a sympathy, or of whom she is quite fond. She withholds information she fears might convict them and, as a result, often finds herself in great danger. Fortunately, Primrose seems to understand this and manages to save her, usually clearing the person she is protecting in the process. Latham's thinking at times can be quite frustrating, and Primrose's method of detecting can be quite mystifying but it is easy to forgive this because things come out all right in the end and it has been a delight to visit such a richly depicted bygone world.

Under the name David Frome, Zenith Brown also wrote a similar series set in England which features Mr. Pinkerton, a rather timid soul who acts and even looks a little like a rabbit. Luckily his domineering wife died, leaving him a very nice pension and no children. He befriends Sgt. Bull of Scotland Yard and is thrilled to help him in any way he can. Like Grace Latham, he feels very ambivalent toward his mentor, often withholding information he is afraid might convict someone he likes. But Bull is usually able to figure out what Pinkerton is hiding and saves the day (and Pinkerton). I find Pinkerton a little pathetic as he seems to have no life of his own and therefore isn't as much fun to read about. Brown also wrote some nonseries books with a very similar modus operandi as she visited different interesting and exotic places. They are a lot of fun to read and, like the works of Mary Roberts Rinehart and Mignon Eberhardt, offer a fine example of popular contemporary American alternatives to Hammett and Chandler.

Kate Mattes

Asia Rip by George Foy (1984)

I remember when I first got *Asia Rip* in the store. The cover is a map of the ocean with a rope and ugly-looking hook lying on top of it and *Asia Rip* written in slashing red letters across it. I thought it was yet another book about drug smuggling and didn't even read the jacket copy. Luckily a customer let me know what I was missing!

Asia Rip is an area of the George's Bank between Nantucket and Cape Cod. Lars Larsen, a commercial fisherman, is the narrator. He and his best friend, Joe (also a fisherman) are about to form a partnership to begin delivering fish straight to the retailer, bypassing the large fishing markets that act as middlemen.

As the book opens on a calm day, Joe sends out an SOS from Asia Rip and then he, his crew and his boat disappear. Lars and Joe's wife, Maria, are the only ones that can't believe it's an accident. Maria, who is pregnant, keeps saying she thinks it is because of their business venture which, if successful, would seriously hamper profits made by the mob in places like the Fulton Fish Market. Lars just knows Joe was too good a fisherman.

Lars soon comes to see that it wasn't an accident. Every time he tries to test a theory, he runs up against roadblocks, threats and then outright violence. Although he has lived and fished the Cape for a long time, he no longer knows who he can trust or where he is safe.

George Foy is a gifted writer. The plot is quite clever. His real strength, however, is in his character development and sense of place. This is a Cape rarely seen by tourists and not even known to all year-rounders. Lars thinks in terms of fishing conditions and fishing markets, and he knows and frequents places most people would avoid. This is a working man's Cape, off season. There are some harrowing underwater scenes and a nail-biting sequence as Lars tries to get off the Cape undetected.

(Imagine a road block at the bridges and you begin to realize the magnitude of this problem.) I'll also tell you that the Fulton Fish Market loses a lot of its charm.

Foy is probably better known as a science fiction writer. He has written another mystery, *Challenger*, which was not as well-plotted, centered around a man who built and sailed his own boat. Again, the strength was in his character development and sense of place. (I liked it and I don't like sailing!) Neither book is in print but keep an eye out for them. They are both New England gems.

Kate Mattes

A Question of Guilt by Frances Fyfield (1988)

Frances Fyfield has been compared to Ruth Rendell, particularly in her ability to bring her intuition to bear on the inner workings of society's psychopathic members. She has also been likened to P.D. James for the ease with which she structures her plots and sets them in their places. She is not unlike Margaret Yorke in her ability to construct a language to encompass the most unpleasant aspects of the evil that men do, and she merits comparison with Elizabeth George in her elegant, yet careful, use of language. But in spite of all the facile comparisons, none is quite on the mark. Fyfield is her own person.

In her first novel, *A Question of Guilt*, she introduces the first of her series protagonists, Crown Prosecutor Helen West and Detective Superintendent Geoffrey Bailey. They are brought together by the actions of Eileen Cartwright, who has taken a perverse interest in her solicitor, Michael Bernard, and thereafter envisions and plots his wife's death. To this end she hires Stanislaus Jaskowski, who first follows the lawyer and then ineptly dispatches the wife. Jaskowski's culpability is apparent and admitted, but it rests with the prosecution to put together the case by which Eileen Cartwright will be brought to account.

Fyfield has developed in Cartwright a fiend of the first order, but even her evil and madness are oddly understandable. A physically unattractive woman, Cartwright was the daughter of a widower with no use for a daughter in general and none for her in particular. But Cartwright has a talent for discovering the merits of discarded furniture and the detritus of home life — recovering for use and for profit those things which are inanimate representations of her life. She has been discarded, unloved by father and husband, remote from feeling life and looking on from afar. Her anger becomes a palpable thing, and frightening. Although in custody for much of the novel, Cartwright is dangerous and far bigger than life.

Helen West and Geoffrey Bailey are less well known by novel's end. Their romance gets set off smartly, and they fit in their comfortable companionship, not remotely ready for the settling down, but willing to experiment with a suspension of their enforced solitariness. Pleasant, yet dedicated to their careers, they each seem subtly uncomfortable with their comfort in a world occupied by the worst elements of the social disorder.

Kathy Phillips

The Paladin by Brian Garfield (1979)

If we had to pick one novel to give to a teenage boy who prefers video games to reading, it would be Brian Garfield's *The Paladin*. Don't get us wrong. *The Paladin* is an adult book and adults are going to love it as well, but it will have special meaning for that young male reader. It's a fantasy — maybe two or three fantasies — that perhaps only a teenage boy can fully appreciate.

The book purports to be a fictionalized account of the exploits of a young British schoolboy who becomes Winston Churchill's personal paladin during World War II. The original paladins were twelve knights who served as Charlemagne's personal warriors. They epitomized courage and loyalty, traits shared by young "Christopher Creighton" (not his real name, Garfield tells us). Although Christopher is only ten when he first meets Churchill in 1935, his independent spirit impresses Churchill. Five years later when Churchill needs to get a spy into Belgium to find out if that (so far) neutral country would stand up against a German attack, he picks Christopher, who takes the code name Christopher Robin. His control is named Winnie-the-Pooh and Churchill becomes (naturally) Tigger.

The idea isn't all that farfetched. And it isn't supposed to be all that dangerous. After all, who would suspect a 15-year-old boy? Christopher is to get himself invited to visit a school chum whose father is a high ranking Belgian official. Told to keep his ears open, Christopher overhears information that can affect Britain's decision whether to stand and fight in France, or evacuate its troops from Dunkirk. But before Christopher can pass on the information to a wireless operator, the German blitzkrieg hits. For the next few days, Christopher makes his way through the fighting, surviving one harrowing encounter after another, before eventually reaching Dunkirk with news that helps save the British army.

Then it's off to Ireland, where Churchill needs to find out if the supposedly neutral Irish are allowing German U-boats to refuel there. Several adult agents have already been killed trying to get the same information, but Churchill again figures no one would suspect a young boy on a cycling vacation. After Ireland it's on to a special school for assassins where Christopher meets up with a woman agent in her twenties who takes him under her wing and eventually into her bed. (Remember what we said about teenage male fantasies?) Upon graduation, Christopher is sent off on several James Bondish missions, including one designed to make sure America comes into the war. Even Churchill is appalled at what Christopher is asked to do. In fact, young Christopher seems to pop up at virtually every critical point — and front — in the war, including the D-day invasion, where once again he plays a pivotal role. By this point we were beginning to suspect Garfield of putting us on, although he insists his story is true and that Christopher was — and is — a remarkable man. In our minds we don't buy this for a minute. But in that special place in the heart where one can still be a teenage boy, we believe every word.

Tom & Enid Schantz

Unpunished by Charlotte Perkins Gilman (1929)

"That man had been killed four times over. Or four ways at once. Possibly five" is the intriguing, pre-*Murder on the Orient Express* conclusion of sleuth Jim Hunt to his lively wife and partner Bess early in *Unpunished*, Charlotte Perkins Gilman's first and only mystery novel. Gilman (1860-1935), great-niece of *Uncle Tom's Cabin* author Harriet Beecher Stowe, is best known for the autobiographical short story "The Yellow Wall-Paper" (1892), now considered a classic feminist work. She wrote *Unpunished*, her final novel, in 1929, but the manuscript languished in Radcliffe's Schlesinger Library until Gilman scholars Catherine J. Golden and Denise D. Knight edited it for publication by Feminist Press in 1997. Unable to publish the novel during her lifetime, Gilman cited as a reason for its failure one publisher's disparaging comment, "I find your characters interesting. That is not necessary in a detective story."

Reinforcing that early cranky reading, Gilman paints an evocative and anguished portrait of an entire household under the thumb of a ruthless blackmailer, Wade Vaughn. All of the suspects have powerful reasons for murder, and Gilman populates her colorful landscape with the resourceful Hunts; their wheelchair-bound but unbowed client Jacqueline Warner; Warner's nosy and informative neighbor Mrs. Todd; and an assortment of lowlifes, sturdy policemen, and honorable servants. While it can be disconcerting to see Italians referred to as "Wops" and African Americans as "colored," all lines converge in two neat and fitting twists at the end.

Gilman described the novel as having "murder enough to satisfy the most demanding, applied in a manner decidedly unusual. It has crime enough for our present day taste, but the criminals are all out of order. There is a pair of most amiable detectives, and another one far from amiable. The mystery involved is not merely in the usual question of who did it, but in the unusual one of who did it first. Some of the tale is amusing."

Gilman may have meant the lively interaction of her offbeat characters; she wrote in *The Forerunner* in September 1913 that "the problem with 'detective stories,' each and all, is that the Plot comes before the People." After all, the root of *Unpunished* is far from a laughfest. In the novel, Gilman prophesied the devastating impact of family abuse that has been more recent grist for the modern judicial mill. While *Unpunished* is undoubtedly a mystery with a message about the effects of an unbridled patriarchy — a recurring theme for Gilman — the reader yearns for more from the Hunt casebook and mourns the passing of this most remarkable pen.

Elizabeth Foxwell

The Tightrope Walker by Dorothy Gilman (1979)

They're going to kill me soon — in a few hours I think — and somehow they'll arrange it so no one will ever guess that I was murdered.

So begins the note Amelia Jones finds in an old hurdy gurdy. Amelia, 22-year-old owner of the Ebbtide Antiques Shop, a shy woman with few friends, is an unlikely detective. But she feels a responsibility to find out what happened to Hannah, the writer of the note. Amelia sees analogies between her efforts to solve this mystery and *The Maze in the Heart of the Castle*, a children's book that "saved her life" after her mother's suicide. *The Maze in the Heart of the Castle* is the story of a quest where the main character confronts danger and evil in a variety of disguises. And Amelia's knowledge of the story turns out to be important in solving the mystery. [Some years later, Gilman wrote a children's book called *The Maze in the Heart of the Castle*. Although it is enjoyable, it doesn't live up to the promise of the sections quoted in *The Tightrope Walker*.]

The Tightrope Walker is both a fine mystery and a well-told story of a woman who learns to trust herself and others. Amelia meets many new people, among them a helpful graphologist, an uninhibited artist's model and an actor and, eventually, two murderers. Amelia finds true love, learns to accept her past and embrace her present. As her guru tells her, "a tree may be bent by harsh winds but it is no less beautiful than the tree that grows in a sheltered nook, and often it bears richer fruit."

Gilman is best known for her Mrs. Pollifax series, which I also recommend. In the first book, *The Unexpected Mrs. Pollifax*, Emily Pollifax, a widow with grown children, is bored with her life and tired of the many volunteer projects that keep her busy. Asked what she wanted to be when she was young, she replies "a spy." Although the questioner laughs, Mrs. Pollifax is inspired to follow her childhood ambition, and applies for a job with the CIA.

Gilman has also written another standalone book that is among my favorites: *The Nun in the Closet*, the story of two nuns who leave their cloister on a mission and encounter illegal drugs, mobsters, hippies and a government agent. All Gilman's protagonists are cheerful and practical in the face of adversity, with a fresh and usual viewpoint that keeps the reader turning pages.

Jennie G. Jacobson

The Zero Trap by Paula Gosling (1979)

Following hard on the heels of her impressive first novel, *A Running Duck*, which was a credible woman-in-jeopardy novel made into a pitiful movie, Paula Gosling came up with a winner in the plot department.

A United States Army plane is hijacked over the Mideast. The plane is found, but the passengers are missing, having been whisked off to the Arctic Circle where they are imprisoned by the subzero weather in a fully outfitted home, including all the amenities right down to a sauna. But who among them is the object of the crime? Or is this the act of madmen with no point other than torment and terror? Among the nine passengers are:

Laura Ainslie, daughter of a three-star general engaged in important negotiations, betrothed to an ambitious Army captain;

Astronomy Professor David Skinner, from a small college in the Midlands, whose brother, a captain in the English navy, is deeply involved in the intrigue of the Cold War spy game;

The angry Sergeant Goade, returning to the States on a three-week leave;

A suspected murderer, Joe Hallick, in the custody of Federal Marshall Denning, on his way back to the US for trial;

Anne and Tom Morgan and their eight-year-old son, Timmy; and

Sherri Lasky, an aging thirtysomething, aware of her sexual allure and not averse to using it to her advantage.

Skinner determines they are in Finland, but to what purpose? Their captors regularly take photographs to show that they are healthy, but can Skinner find a way to communicate their whereabouts? And when one of their number meets death by violence, they suspect that the death may unsettle the kidnappers' goals and lead to all their deaths — so they must engage in a frightening and ghoulish deception.

Even after repeated readings, and in spite of the removal of the Cold War threats from our imaginings, *The Zero Trap* retains its freshness. The solution is elegant, convoluted and breathtaking. That such a tour-de-force of suspense should have sunk without a trace is nothing short of tragedy.

Kathy Phillips

Beyond a Reasonable Doubt by C.W. Grafton (1950)

Cornelius Warren Grafton's last mystery, *Beyond a Reasonable Doubt*, is considered by many to be a classic. In 1976 it was included in the "Fifty Classics of Crime Fiction" edited by Jacques Barzun and Wendell Hertig Taylor, who said that "the originality of the novel lies in the superbly maintained suspense of the first person narrative and even more to the extraordinary ingenuity with which the details of the true and falsified sequence of events are dovetailed."

Grafton (yes, he is Sue Grafton's father) was born in China where his parents were missionaries. He came to the United States to study and in 1931 received a degree in journalism from Columbia University. He taught English literature for several years, intending to return to China as a missionary, but at his brother's urging, he attended law school and practiced law in Louisville, Kentucky.

In *Beyond a Reasonable Doubt*, a young lawyer, Jess London, kills his abusive and thoroughly despicable brother-in-law, Mitch Southern. When his sister becomes prime suspect, he confesses. The story is structured around the way Jess first convinces the unbelieving homicide detective, Lieutenant Richmond, that he is guilty and then in court pleads not guilty and defends himself. Jon Breen, in *Novel Verdicts,* called it "one of the most cleverly plotted and suspenseful trial novels of them all."

The story begins with a detailed description of the events of the 24 hours before the body is discovered. The prose is exceptionally spontaneous and bright for such a detailed narrative. It is very hard to describe the storyline without making it sound incredibly laborious but it is far from confusing or dry. After presenting the details of who said what when and who saw whom when and what happened to what hat and when the tear in the pants appeared and was mended, Jess London explains to the police exactly what happened. He quickly discovers that the police have evidence that that is not what happened. They dismiss his confession as an effort to protect his sister, thereby strengthening the case against her.

Eventually Jess does get to court where he defends himself, needing to prove not that he is innocent, but that there is reasonable doubt. If I could describe that scene, I would have written the book. It comprises 40% of the story.

Reading this book is like watching a Billy Wilder film with a young Cary Grant and Katherine Hepburn. Set in 1940, it is filled with ironic description, smart conversation and self-deprecating, wise-ass humor. One snappy comment leads to another. It could only be filmed in black and white; technicolor would distract from the ingenious way Grafton uses truth against itself to create false impressions in service of a good cause — himself.

Sharon Villines

The Leavenworth Case: A Lawyer's Story by Anna Katharine Green (1878)

The Leavenworth Case became the first bestselling book in history. At 32, Anna Katharine Green became an instant success in both America and Europe and by her death in 1935, the book had sold over a million copies.

Yale used *The Leavenworth Case* as a text. Stanley Baldwin praised it in the House of Lords. Wilkie Collins wrote admiringly of it. Arthur Conan Doyle corresponded with Green and made a special trip to meet her. Writers like Mary Roberts Rinehart and John Dickson Carr acknowledged her influence. Agatha Christie remembered the story being read to her as a child and in *The Clocks* (1963), Poirot praises its period atmosphere, deliberate melodrama, lavish descriptions and excellent psychological study of the murderer.

But while Green's accomplishments and influence were well recognized by her contemporaries, Green has been largely ignored since the 1930s.

The story is a blend of romance, police procedural and legal thriller. The daughter of a prominent Manhattan defense attorney and friend of the New York City chief of police, Green grew up listening to discussions of criminal cases, rules of evidence and methods of investigation. She balances romance and melodrama with rational explanations. The uniquely American characters and settings include careful studies of class and ethnicity.

The story begins with the discovery of the body of millionaire Horatio Leavenworth in the locked library where he had gone to write a new will disinheriting one of his two beautiful wards, Mary and Eleanore, for a suspected deficiency of character. Unlike the thin hawk-eyed detectives then popular, the homicide detective Ebenezer Gryce is portly, wise and human. Like Columbo, he appears distracted but is always on the job. The narrator is a young attorney who is asked by Gryce to help him investigate in a social milieu where Gryce is neither comfortable nor welcome. Both women become suspects and the attorney, of course, falls in love.

The elements of *The Leavenworth Case* became essential to the work of the great British writers: the rich man killed before signing a new will, a body in the library, the dignified butler, medical evidence on the cause and time of death, the coroner's inquest with testimony of expert witnesses, ballistics evidence, maps, torn fragments of a letter, newspaper headlines tracking the case, lists of deductions and questions, and even the final gathering of suspects to confront the killer.

In over 30 novels in 45 years, Green not only laid the

groundwork for the Golden Age, she created the prototypes for almost all of the detective types including a shrewd, wealthy, middle-aged spinster with whom Gryce forms an ambiguous attachment; Amelia Butterworth, who becomes the prototype for Miss Marple and Maud Silver; and the debutante-paid-to-investigate "New Woman" detective, Violet Strange, the prototype for Nancy Drew and Hilda Adams.

As mother of three, an avid gardener and the primary support of her family including a mother-in-law and a sister, Green remained Victorian. She did not support suffrage or adopt post-war dress. This surely contributed to her decline in popularity but the decline in critical attention is bewildering.

Sharon Villines

Not a Creature Was Stirring by Jane Haddam (1990)

Not a Creature Was Stirring marks the first in a delightful series centering on the retired FBI specialist Gregor Demarkian and on Cavanaugh Street, an Armenian-American community in Philadelphia. Not cozy, but not hardboiled, this series can be read by all and should be.

Two problems arise. First, Robert Hannaford is murdered right before Gregor arrives for dinner. Second, Donna Moradanyan is pregnant and the father is missing. Characterization, sense of place and an excellent plot combine to make this an unusually fine book. Very few mysteries written today display all three of these elements. Humor is also present even though the books deal with serious issues and nasty crimes.

Characterization is excellent because the characters are realistic and have both strengths and weaknesses. Gregor is still mourning the long illness and death of his wife two years after it occurred. His barren life is epitomized by the description of his apartment.

Jane Haddam builds characterization based on these actions of everyday life. When Gregor and Father Tibor go out to lunch, "Gregor wondered what was going through his mind. Maybe he'd spent so much of his life dealing with big evils, the little ones had escaped his notice."

Bennis Hannaford, bestselling author of a successful fantasy series, becomes both a murder suspect and a main character in the series. She moves away from the WASP environment in which she was raised and into an apartment on Cavanaugh Street. She too has been lonely, and now begins to seek a richer life among the interesting characters in this Armenian neighborhood. This neighborhood is marked by an extremely strong sense of place. Cavanaugh Street is an old-fashioned and yet modern Armenian enclave where neighbors still care about one another. It is the older women and Father Tibor, an Eastern Orthodox priest who suffered greatly under the communist regime, who hold the street together. When Donna Moradanya becomes pregnant, the entire street becomes involved in taking care of her and Gregor becomes involved in finding the father of her child.

The murder of Bennis Hannaford's father is followed by the murder of one of his daughters. The life in a stultifying Bryn Mawr mansion is eloquently described. It is difficult to elucidate the complexity of the plot without giving away too much of it. The novel ends with an epilog on Epiphany in which characters are shown to have grown, thus fulfilling the promise of this church festival. They will continue to grow during the rest of the series, and Cavanaugh Street will remain a strong character in its own right.

Anne Poe Lehr

Dog in the Dark by Gerald Hammond (1989)

Dog in the Dark is the first of Gerald Hammond's John Cunningham series. Major John Cunningham has been invalided out of the Army not because of a bullet, as his neighbors insist on believing, but rather because of a pernicious and debilitating bug that has defied diagnosis or cure. He has been living with his brother and dabbling in handling his springer spaniel at field trials when, in spite of the malaise generated by his illness, Cunningham finds himself talked into running a breeding and training kennel for springer spaniels by a nosy but well-meaning field trials judge who introduces him to Isobel Kitts. She becomes his partner.

Three Oaks is barely set up when John comes across a violent confrontation practically in his back yard. Two village women, housewife breeders of spaniels for show, are faced off against a local farmer who has shot one of their dogs for worrying the sheep — a justifiable shooting in the eyes of Scottish law. When John refuses to back the women in their denial that the dog worried the sheep he makes three enemies. When one of the women is found murdered John feels he's a suspect and decides to investigate.

The books are in the first person and the conflicts always center around the kennel and those who come to it for dogs or training and those, for various reasons, who wish John ill and come to do him or his property harm.

There is much about dogs, guns, field trials and hunting, all of it fascinating and cleverly woven into the story while moving it forward. It is obvious that many of those whom John encounters care more about their dogs than about people (not a bad thing in my book). Hammond's love of the Scottish countryside is evident in his descriptions (never overdone) and his wit and turn of phrase will have you smiling, sometimes with a tear in your eye.

Cunningham's flawed character is very appealing. Isobel's

penchant for drink is nicely balanced with her skills as a veterinarian and dog handler and her obvious devotion to the kennel, to John and to her husband, Henry, who provides a cogent mind and a wide array of business contacts when an investigation is in progress. Beth, originally hired as a kennel maid, proves herself invaluable to the partnership both in her willingness to work and her logical and clever mind. In fact, while John is the one who seems to attract the mayhem and initiates the investigations, it is usually Beth who sees the way to the solution. Their relationship grows quickly from employer/ employee to that of lovers, husband and wife, and then parents.

Sally Powers

With a Bare Bodkin by Cyril Hare (1946)

Of the nine mystery novels of Cyril Hare, *Tragedy at Law* and *An English Murder* have been the most celebrated, and justly so. However, *With a Bare Bodkin*, with its air of whimsicality and fantasy, is a novel of singularity and distinction. That during the war a large bureaucracy should be necessary to oversee the production of pins is in itself rather fantastic.

Three patterns in the novel begin to evolve quickly. Francis Pettigrew is sent north to Marsett Bay, on the very fringes of "our nook-shotten island," to act as legal counsel for the Pin Control. He observes several employees, who, having discovered that a fellow worker, a Mr. Wood, has written mystery novels, seek to enliven their routine by creating a fiction, a plot to murder the Controller. They imagine the villain to be Miss Danville, a fellow worker given to fantasies induced by religious mania. This creation of fictions within a fiction allows Hare to play with the vagaries of human imagination, to poke fun at writers ("all writers are a bit cracked"), to comment on the structures of mystery plots, and to write a kind of bibliomystery. As the workers sneak time to rehearse in the building's corridors, the plot begins to seem more real than fiction. Hare plays with the idea that the human "craving for melodrama" creates fictions, and that realities and unrealities seem to merge and blend.

Meanwhile Pettigrew meets Inspector Mallett, on special assignment to investigate leakage of information about pins and possible black market activities. When Miss Danville is murdered with a bodkin, a long skewer used for making holes in paper, Mallett and Pettigrew are at difficulties to connect the two cases. Was the plot created to enable a real murder to take place? Did Danville know something about leaked information, about the missing Blenkinsop file?

The novel is complicated by a love interest, as Pettigrew's secretary, a Miss Brown whom he has just met, is being courted by Mr. Phillips, a man much her senior. Pettigrew, fearing that Phillips is married, conducts a surreptitious investigation, revealing that Phillips' wife is dead. When Phillips pressures Miss Brown to insure her life, Pettigrew imagines another murder may take place. Pettigrew and Mallett discover that the murderer created a fiction accepted as a reality by the world.

That the mildly gloomy Pettigrew himself is falling in love is handled by Hare with great restraint. Pettigrew's recognition that he loves his new secretary recalls a similar passage in Jane Austen's *Pride and Prejudice*, where Elizabeth Bennett performs a similarly ruthless self-analysis. Pettigrew's proposal is as excoriating a summing up of personal characteristics as is found in fiction, and certainly ranks as one of the strangest, and most honest, proposals in literary history.

This novel's mixture of reality and imaginative fantasy is a delightful exploration of fictions, with its detectives, villains and lovers. No wonder Shakespearean allusions abound.

Gordon Magnuson

The Last Known Address by Joseph Harrington (1965)

Arguably the finest police procedural ever written, *The Last Known Address* offers a page-turning investigative exercise in its purest form. Strictly speaking, *Last Known Address* isn't even a crime novel: New York City Police Sergeant Frank Kerrigan and his novice partner Jane Boardman are simply trying to locate a missing witness for a mob prosecution. Yet as Joseph Harrington follows their subterranean progress from borough to borough, asking question after question, crossing off one dead end after another, he creates a compelling picture of a pair of cops, a city and an era.

Little about *Last Known Address* is truly innovative, yet everything about the story feels fresh. Typically, the police come across as honest, hard-working and unimaginative, while the DA is politically ambitious and too responsive to pressure from City Hall. Kerrigan is a former detective who arrested the wrong influential citizen and was busted down to walking a beat on Staten Island. Boardman is naïve and pretty, hired (her cynical male colleagues correctly assume) as "masher-bait." No one expects them to find the missing witness, who has brilliantly eluded earlier investigators, though Kerrigan's captain knows enough about the man's tenacity and intelligence to cherish faint hopes of their success.

The novel thus attractively combines a number of elements common to detective fiction: the "cold case," the disgraced cop seeking redemption, the senior officer teaching a neophyte the ropes. It's a suspenseful book (the witness must be found within the week) and a neat puzzler: how does an ordinary citizen hide from the law and the mob? Kerrigan's stolid brilliance emerges as he methodically asks all the questions that were asked before, and then asks just one more.

For writers later in the century, such as the Swedish team of Maj Sjöwall and Per Wallöö, procedurals served as satiric tools, exposing the absurdity of a dehumanizing bureaucracy, but for

Harrington, the procedural celebrates ordinary life and the routines we all follow. In a series of interviews with moving men, teachers, secretaries and pharmacists, Harrington portrays a cross-section of working New Yorkers. As they do their jobs — teach children, take shorthand dictation, fill out delivery forms — these citizens also record, indirectly, the life of the missing man. Kerrigan's success, we realize, derives in large part from his respect for other people's labor. As he asks about their routines, listens to their stories, he ultimately learns about his quarry. Yet despite this positive view of police work, *The Last Known Address* doesn't paint a simplistically rosy picture, and finding the witness ultimately injures at least one innocent victim.

Harrington wrote two other excellent Kerrigan novels, *Blind Spot* and *The Last Doorbell*; the latter is particularly compelling and painful (the criminal is a sexual predator of children). Beside any of these novels, most contemporary procedurals seem turgid and bloated. Harrington's economical narrative (the brief novel originally appeared in Redbook) reminds us that a good police story doesn't require self-indulgent details of the protagonists' private lives, graphic depictions of violence or culturally validating lists of consumer goods. It's enough to have a cop we care about, a puzzle worth solving and a disciplined writer who can bring both to life.

Lisa Berglund

The Christening Day Murders by Lee Harris (1993)

Christine Bennett is a former nun who lives outside of New York City where she works as a part-time teacher. A good bit of her time is spent taking care of her home and her policeman boyfriend, and helping her friends solve problems. She is at home one afternoon when she receives a call from an old school mate announcing that the friend has had a baby boy who will be christened at the church in a town that no longer exists.

Thirty years ago the government bought up all of the property and evacuated the town of Studsburg, then flooded it. This was done to create a much needed reservoir. The last child to be baptized there was Chris' friend Mattie. Now because of a drought the town has been uncovered and the church is found still standing. Mattie contacts the priest who baptized her and gets him to agree to the baptism of her son. Chris is very excited about attending. She arrives early. After walking around the remains of the town, located about one hundred and fifty miles north of New York City, she goes to the church. Chris is wandering around inside the church when she hears a noise in the basement. Upon further investigation she makes a gruesome discovery: the skeletal remains of a body that has been there for 30 years.

The sheriff's deputies from the next town are called to investigate the body. As long as the television cameras are there, they are actively investigating. When the cameras disappear so do the deputies. Chris thinks this is a golden opportunity to get involved. She begins by asking Mattie's parents about the day of her christening. Mattie was born just before the Fourth of July and her parents asked the engineers if they would hold off the flooding of the town so that Mattie could be baptized and the town could celebrate one more Fourth. The baptism took place, the picnic was held, they had fireworks and everyone said goodbye. Chris locates the former mayor, newspaper owner and some of the other people who lived in the town. She also interviews the priest. With the aid of her boyfriend and the Mother Superior at her convent she finally figures it out.

Lee Harris has written thirteen books in this series, each with a different premise. This one is special to me because Lee dedicated this one to me.

Paige Rose

The Edge of the Crazies by Jamie Harrison (1995)

If you travel to Blue Deer, Montana for a little rest and relaxation, you'd better watch your back. When you hear something sneaking up on you, use extreme caution; it might be a bear, but it's more likely to be your neighbor. I'm not entirely sure which is worse.

Edge of the Crazies is the debut book in Jamie Harrison's well-reviewed yet commercially overlooked series about a small town in rural Montana. The title refers not only to the geographic location of the town (nestled in the Crazy Mountains), but also to the hamlet's inhabitants, who are nursing more grudges than a county with a population of 12,000 can possibly hold. The lunatic running the asylum is Sheriff Jules Clement, a born and bred local boy who is related to half the town and more accustomed to breaking the law than enforcing it. After traversing the world as an archeologist, Jules had a hankering for the prairie, and returned home to fill his long-dead father's shoes as the local law. He's been regretting it ever since.

Blue Deer is a quiet town, where the criminal element indulges in domestic violence, car thefts and bar brawls at the cheerfully seedy Blue Bat Bar (the local drink of choice is a "whisky ditch" — whisky, water and your probable destination). So when nouveau riche hack screenwriter George Blackwater gets his office (and himself) peppered with rifle bullets, the town is abuzz with theories. The most popular hypotheses center on either George's wife or his mistress as the amateur sniper; both are considered "tirebiters" in the local vernacular (large, troublesome women), and both live up to their moniker. Jules has never worked a major crime before; the worst incident he has witnessed was an elderly farmer devoured by his own swine, and in that case the culprits were obvious. It's up to our laconic hero to wade through the town's collective animosities and find George's assailant, while the body count keeps rising.

The genius of this book is that the writing style is laid back, yet sharp — just like Jules. Harrison deftly explores the contradiction of a town that is a vacation playground for the wealthy and tacky, but also fiercely Western and blue collar. Tensions rise between the long-time locals and their nemeses, the rich out-of-towners, who stay long enough to sully Blue Deer but not long enough to pay taxes. This volatile mix is always bubbling beneath the surface of the town, often with hilarious results. But animosity is not just reserved for the Gucci-shod interlopers; there's an awful lot of homegrown malice going around as well. One thing is for sure: both the indigenous and imported wildlife are mighty dangerous.

This mystery is intelligent, well-plotted and highly original, as are the three that follow it. Harrison has many pointed and witty insights into small town life, and her dialog and whimsical cast of characters reflect her confident and imaginative style. Why is this series so underappreciated? I couldn't say. I'll tell you this, though: when someone walks into Murder Ink, and asks for a well written, entertaining mystery with sophisticated humor, this is what I give them. And they always come back for the second one.

I think it's time for a whisky ditch right about now.

Melanie Meyers Cushman

Lonely Hearts by John Harvey (1989)

When I first decided to write about John Harvey's *Lonely Hearts*, the first in his series featuring Nottingham policeman Charlie Resnick, I thought I'd just glance at the beginning and maybe read a couple of chapters to refresh my memory on some details. Instead, I found myself immediately caught up, ensnared really, in the story, the writing, and the characters all over again. I thought it was exceptional the first time I read it; rereading it this time, with the bittersweet satisfaction of having a complete series to reflect on (Harvey ended it with the tenth book), *Lonely*

Hearts stands out even more as exceptional, both on its own, and as the beginning of a remarkable series.

All the elements of the ideal mystery are here: evocative yet relatively spare writing, characters both believable and memorable, and a plot that uses a realistic crime-solving story to make a larger point about philosophical issues of good and evil, moral decisions, and the socioeconomic underpinnings of crime. Born to Polish immigrant parents, Resnick is somewhat of an outsider and thus perhaps both more observant and willing to think "outside the box" when it comes to crime-solving. He is also a compassionate loner, somewhat resigned yet still hoping when it comes to relationships, and a lover of jazz, his four cats and messy sandwiches. In the hands of a less skilled writer, this combination would become the quirky hero so prevalent in contemporary mysterydom. But Resnick is so real, I expect to see him behind me in the deli or flipping through the rare CD rack at the music store.

The members of his CID team are similarly memorable, deftly defined in just a sentence or two: The ambitious and prissily by-the-book sergeant who doesn't understand why his annoying self-righteousness is not leading to promotion: "Graham Millington had a small hand mirror propped up on his desk and was using a pair of nail scissors to trim his moustache." A shallow, sexist constable: "The world divided into three equal parts: you drank it, fly-tackled it or got your leg over it."

In *Lonely Hearts,* women are being killed by a man they apparently meet through personal ads. Update this part to Internet dating and the book could have been written today, while the themes of urban grime, despair and loneliness are timeless. However, this is not to say that this book, or any in the series, is relentlessly depressing or humorless. Resnick has a wry sensibility and skewers his straight-arrow superiors, at least in his thoughts: "...everything that came across his desk was dated and filed, each phone call logged, he probably had the paper clips sorted according to colour and weight... He breathed tightly, as if begrudging the air."

Maybe Harvey's series is particularly satisfying to American readers because he deliberately set out to "present American readers with a series of crime novels which are set in a real British world" [Interview in Deadly Pleasures Issue 7, pp. 35-37]. Although Harvey's frame of reference is post-Thatcherite Britain, it's easy to apply the analogies to contemporary American society.

Maria Parker

A Comedy of Murders by George Herman (1994)

I recently told a friend of a novel set in late fifteenth century Italy. I said that the plot had quite a lot to do with the "commedia dell'arte" (which I have come to think of as Renaissance improv), and he replied, "that's such an obscure subject, I'm not surprised it didn't sell well in the States." I tell you now what I told him: this book is your chance to learn some history, and in a most entertaining method.

A Comedy of Murders features a troupe of itinerant actors, I Comici Buffoni; Duke Ludovico Sforza of Milan, "Il Moro," and his court; Maestro Leonardo da Vinci, artist-engineer; Niccolo, a dwarf; and various other nobles, cardinals, envoys, ministers, security personnel and peasants. George Herman, who knows a thing or two about the history of theater as well as Renaissance Italy, has plotted this book beautifully, in the manner of a fine tapestry. Not a thread is out of place. It was a delight to reread this book after several years: I was pleasantly surprised to find myself appreciating the storylines, characterizations and clever dialog even more than I did the first time.

Throughout the story Niccolo may be found reading from the book of the Greek philosopher Epictetus. Soon after saving the life of Il Moro, and being invited to live at the Duke's court,

Niccolo finds himself waylaid and put to work as a spy for the Countess Bergamini. The text he reads that day is pertinent to the situation in which Niccolo finds himself: "remember that you are an actor in a play, of such sort as the divine Author chooses. Play it appropriately. Your duty is to act well the part assigned. The crafting of the plot, however, is another's."

Everyone, it seems, has enemies and murders abound, no two committed in the same manner. Late in the story Niccolo sighs over what he sees as a tragedy, the murder of an innocent young woman. Maestro Leonardo's response to him interested me:

You value youth above life? Or social status? Is it less a tragedy when an old man is murdered? The fact, my young friend, is that murder is never a tragedy. Nothing is ever resolved by murder. All the motives — a consolidation of power, an acquisition of wealth or property, the avenging of another murder — none of these have any permanent effect. Power shifts. Wealth buys nothing of lasting value. The vendettas here in the castle should teach you that one murder does not wipe away another but multiplies it! No. No. A murderer is a fool, and the proper place for a fool is not in a tragedy, but in a comedy.

Ah, but George Herman is not a fool! If the reader becomes less foolish, and more knowledgeable, about history, logic, philosophy, mathematics, tears and laughter, then perhaps Herman's novel was not published in vain.

Amy Proni

Envious Casca by Georgette Heyer (1941)

Georgette Heyer (1902-1974) is justly famed for her exquisite Regency novels, tales that elegantly continue the tradition of the "comedy of manners" set by Jane Austen. Two of these romances, *The Talisman Ring* and *The Corinthian*, delightfully combine romance with murder. Most or all of her romances are in print or easily available in used book stores — but that is not as true of her twelve mysteries. Why?

Four of these mysteries form a series featuring Superintendent Hannasyde, and then his associate, Inspector Hemingway, takes over for another four. The remaining range from a historical mystery to traditional 1930s Golden Age country-house mayhem and murder.

Envious Casca, written during WWII, is the second in the later series. The tale begins on Christmas Eve and is set in a drafty mansion owned by the elderly (and inevitably) cantankerous Nicholas Herriard. Nat grudgingly shares the house with his sprightly brother Joe, an impecunious former thespian of few talents and many histrionics, and Joe's wife, who blends into the furniture while reading biographies of minor royalty.

Various relations and significant others begin arriving for the festivities, welcomed by a nauseatingly cheery Joe and a gouty Nathaniel.

The cast of characters is the usual eclectic group of people that get together in the vast majority of country house thrillers of that era.

There is a vivid niece who can match Joe histrionic for histrionic; her escort, an insecure (and lower-class) playwright; a contentious nephew and his shrilly vulgar girlfriend; and Nat's insecure business partner. With pleasure the reader welcomes the voice of reason and sanity in the character of a distant cousin, who is a contemporary of the younger set.

The stage is now set as this ill-assorted household prepares for Christmas and ends up with murder — in a locked room no less!

Heyer's biographer, Jane Aiken Hodge, feels that the spirit that makes so many of her Regencies so magical is missing from her mysteries, partially because Heyer's barrister husband worked with her on the plots of the detective stories, and perhaps because Heyer was also hampered by the dictates of the Golden Age. In short, the dictates of a historical society and Almacks suit Heyer far more than the contemporary rules imposed upon mystery writers in the '30s and '40s.

However, while her plots are standard, her denouements never cheat the reader. The murderer in *Envious Casca* is a clever and logical surprise.

Aside from the plots, the dialog in Heyer's mysteries sparkles and her characters break from the formula, standing sturdily on their own in the reader's mind. Heyer was, after all, a contemporary of Noel Coward's.

Now these mysteries are becoming available on audio tape, and together with the magical Regency romances, form a body of work that is uniquely designed to delight a reader with lost eras wherein love does indeed conquer all — and so delightfully!

Josephine Bayne

Falling Angel by William Hjortsberg (1978)

There are many books for which you have such fond and loving memories that you don't want to reread them. The fear is that the book simply can't be as good as you remember. I was therefore very reluctant to pick up *Falling Angel* again, an Edgar nominee for best first mystery and one of my all-time favorites. But the book was every bit as good as I remember it.

I first read *Falling Angel* 12 years ago while working at the wonderful, but sadly closed, Foul Play bookstore in New York City. I remember that when copies of the book arrived, a colleague took one look at the cover of this particular paperback edition and dismissed the book as a horror story, wanting to return it immediately. Luckily for my customers and me the books were rescued and this classic private eye story was always one of our best sellers.

Harry Angel of the Crossroads Detective Agency takes on a missing persons job in New York City in the late 1950s. Within a few pages you know that this is a bizarre, unique story because on Friday the 13th, Harry meets Lewis Cypher in the restaurant located at 666 Fifth Avenue. Cypher hires Harry to find Johnny Favorite, a popular crooner from the 1940s. Favorite had been badly injured in World War II and had recently disappeared from the private hospital that cared for him for many years. Angel follows the trail of Favorite through an underworld of voodoo, witchcraft and black magic. At the end Angel not only confronts the truth about himself but the truth about his employer.

There are so many pleasures in this clever novel. Unlike many mainstream writers who dabble in detective fiction, William Hjortsberg has perfect pitch for writing the first person narrative of a private eye and he plots with a simple elegance. He captures the feel of the city during the Eisenhower years from the smoke rings of the Camel sign in Times Square to the jazz clubs in Harlem to the funhouses of Coney Island. And a sprinkling of humor (would you hire a law firm named McIntosh, Winesap and Spy?) lightens the darkness of the story.

I was very pleased when *Falling Angel* came back into print five years ago and I recommend it highly to anyone who wants a mystery that is out of the ordinary.

Bonnie Claeson

Midnight Baby by Wendy Hornsby (1993)

When an author begins a new series, one of the seminal decisions is the framework the character operates within. The decision of amateur versus professional sleuth ultimately determines the level of belief we readers engage each time we open the pages of a new book. Wendy Hornsby introduced her investigative filmmaker Maggie MacGowen to crime solving via a case involving a family member in *Telling Lies*. Over the 1990s, four more Maggie novels followed, including *Midnight Baby*. Maggie is the best sort of amateur sleuth, combining a job that doesn't stretch suspension of disbelief excessively with the sort of personality that seeks answers and justice. Because the character's career is the image behind the lens, readers are able to view the same reality Maggie brings to her documentaries, and her sense of passion and compassion, most compelling in *Midnight Baby*, which can be considered the cornerstone in this series.

Maggie is from the Bay area, but most of the books are set in Los Angeles, giving her a different perspective on the City of Angels. She is a single mother who balances a demanding job, time with her children, and her personal life while recognizing she is making sacrifices in each area. Maggie emerged at about the same time as Jan Burke's reporter Irene Kelly, and holds a similar appeal for readers.

It is hard to pin down what makes *Midnight Baby* stand out in particular. Sure, it has a great story line, dealing with the marginalized teens of America's urban landscape. It has a lot of heart, as Maggie is drawn to the victim through perceived similarities to her own daughter. It has a nice balance of the sleuth working with, not in opposition to, the police as they investigate the murder. A particular strength in Hornsby's writing is her believable dialog, particularly between Maggie and her cop boyfriend, Mike Flynn, and the balance they must maintain between their professional and personal lives. But none of the individual components are unique, whether in comparison to Hornsby's other works or others in the field. What sets *Midnight Baby* apart is that indefinable something special that happens when a talented author's writing transcends the sum of the parts, making the whole a special product, one which carries emotional resonance far beyond the solution of the crime and the closing of the book.

Maggie's character continues to grow in complexity in a

very realistic fashion over the course of the next several books, *Bad Intent*, *77th Street Requiem* and *A Hard Light*, without ever losing its appeal to readers who want a strong, competent and caring protagonist.

Hornsby wrote two earlier mysteries, and received multiple awards for her work. Her Edgar winning short story, "Nine Sons," packs a huge emotional punch. She is a professor at Long Beach City College.

Maryelizabeth Hart & Elizabeth Baldwin

Bridge of Birds by Barry Hughart (1984)

In order to bankrupt the entire village of Ku-fu and put all the peasants in debt to them for all eternity, Pawnbroker Fang and Ma the Grub poison the mulberry leaves that will be fed to the silk worms. As they hoped, all the silk worms die. At the same time, though, all the children in the village between the ages of eight and thirteen — including Pawnbroker Fang's daughter Fawn — fall prey to some unknown plague that sends them into a coma. Number Ten Ox — whose real name is Lu Yu — is sent to the city of Peking to find someone who can explain to the village how a plague could learn to count. He returns with Li Kao, a sage with a slight flaw in his character. Thus begins an insane joyride through Chinese history, tradition, culture and myth.

Bridge of Birds (subtitled "A Novel of an Ancient China That Never Was") — and its two sequels, *The Story of the Stone* and *Eight Skilled Gentlemen* — is a mystery wrapped in an infinite number of capers. In fact, the capers so take over the story that it isn't until much later in the book that you realize they are camouflaging the actual mystery. Even when I was reading the third book in the series and thought myself reasonably familiar with Hughart's *modus operandi*, I still fell into the trap of letting the capers sidetrack me — which is not that hard because they are so delightfully imaginative.

Hughart's masterful stinginess with his characters, scenes, props and even words would make even Miser Shen swoon with admiration. There is no such thing as a "throw away" character or "filler" action in Hughart's universe. It may take two hundred pages, but each character will eventually play a part in the main mystery, and every action will be fully explained. The solutions to all three mysteries only seem to fall out of the clear blue sky; in reality the groundwork was laid from the very first page, and a second reading will have you muttering, "How did I miss *that*?"

Eight Skilled Gentlemen, the third and last of the series, was published back in 1988. I've asked around, but nobody seems to know what Hughart is up to these days or whether he's still writing. I certainly hope so. I would hate to think that such a talented writer with such an incredibly inventive imagination has said all he intends to say.

Kate Birkel

Before the Fact by Francis Iles (1932)

Before the Fact is a riveting study in innocence, creeping terror, narcissism unleashed and twisted love. It is a psychological look at a potential murderer as seen through the eyes of his intended victim.

Publisher and critic Bennett Cerf believed its first paragraph to be the most perfect introduction to a murder story he ever read. And this statement was made some thirteen years after it was first published.

Although set in the somnolent English countryside of the late 1920s, the crimes and characters of *Before the Fact* could as easily be found in your hometown, this week. It's all so plausible — and all the more frightening because of that.

Clever Lina McLaidlaw is nearly 30 and unmarried when

she meets handsome Johnnie Aysgarth at a countryside picnic. He is her constant and flattering companion that afternoon. Lina believes that because she is not pretty, she is a failure as a woman. And she very much wants to be married. Johnnie, with his reputation as a rotter, sweeps clever Lina off her feet in spite of his rudeness and excuses for poor behavior. She forgives him, she madly adores him. Never sure of herself or Johnnie, she is passionately grateful when he marries her.

Life with Johnnie is exasperating. He cheats waiters, he leases a house twice as large as they need, he gambles without control. Lina succumbs to his glib but vague excuses, his flattery and his promises to reform. But Johnnie doesn't reform. He has affair after affair, he steals from the neighbors and embezzles from his employer. Lina covers his debts, turns a blind eye to his romances and grows to feel that only she understands him and can keep him out of trouble. Keeping Johnnie out of trouble becomes her total consuming responsibility.

"Lina Aysgarth had lived with her husband for eight years before she realized that she was married to a murderer." But what can she do? It is not a straightforward murder. Really not a murder at all. Certainly unfortunate circumstances are involved, and perhaps intent. And certainly Johnnie benefits from the death, but still…

Lina's fears, indecision and insecurity along with Johnnie's charm, insouciance and blarney finally lead Johnnie to one last murder — and Lina knowingly becomes an accessory before the fact.

You know from the first sentence that Johnnie Aysgarth is a murderer. You don't know until the last chapter just how without conscience he is. Every sentence, every paragraph between the first and the last builds your understanding of the motivations of both Lina and Johnnie, how they think and feel and move through their lives. Each incident builds on the one before until there is only one possible outcome for them both.

Although nothing is hidden along the way that last chapter still stuns you with its force. This one is not to be missed.

The 1941 RKO release *Suspicion* by Alfred Hitchcock, starring Cary Grant and Joan Fontaine, was based on Francis Iles' *Before the Fact*. Hitchcock always picked the best.

Kathleen Riley

Panicking Ralph by Bill James (1997)

Bill James is the best living mystery writer. His Harpur & Iles series is without parallel. *Panicking Ralph* provides scintillating insight into the criminal mind. Of course, the criminal thoughts are not confined to the lawbreakers.

The story opens with Ralph Ember (aka Panicking Ralph) enjoying a "romantic" beach interlude with his girlfriend, Christine. The approach of two thugs sends Ralph and Christine hightailing it across the deserted foreshore. Ralph is faster and Christine falls victim. Ralph's chivalry is limited to a belated attempt to lovingly dispose of the corpse.

The local drug czar, Oliphant Kenward Knapp, has recently undergone an untimely demise. Panicking Ralph forms a syndicate to take up the slack. Naturally, there is a rival local syndicate, and there are overtures from established firms in London. The maneuvering and posturing form the backdrop for this post-modern urban game of musical chairs. Ralph teams up with Harry Foster and Gerry Reid. Keith Vine aligns himself with Stanley Stanfield. There is a wonderful scene of body disposal at sea that evokes Laurel and Hardy more than Raymond Chandler.

The fascinating aspect of this view of current underworld struggle is the frank participation and involvement of the police. Detective Chief Superintendent Colin Harpur and Assistant Chief Constable Desmond Iles are the closest to protagonists that James has to offer. The interplay between

Harpur and Iles lies at the heart of the entire series. Harpur is the large, disheveled, well-intentioned plodder and Iles the small, dandy, pragmatic Machiavelli. Their verbal exchanges are priceless. It's like being ringside to a sparring session between Dorothy Parker and Oscar Wilde. James' gift for dialog is extraordinary. Each word is a gem to be scrutinized and worshipped. On not-so-rare occasions, I'll burst out laughing. Nero Wolfe and Archie Goodwin have been displaced at the pinnacle of mystery duos.

Ralph is a continuing miscreant in the series. His hated title, Panicking, stems from his propensity for panic attacks when under pressure. He feels as if his jaw line scar is weeping during his frequent periods of high stress. Readers are treated to his frenetic paranoia and squirrelly planning. It's reminiscent of the depraved thinking of Flashman from the classic series by George Macdonald Fraser.

All of the criminals in James' fictional English city have pretensions to gentility. Ralph's manor residence is named Low Pastures. He owns a drinking club named the Monty. While it seems that all of the patrons are crooks, there are gestures towards elegance. Each action is considered only in the context of appearances. The police are much more practical. They come from the "ends justify the means" school. This parody of the upper class runs throughout the series. Only the crooks try to do the right thing.

I've recommended this series to all of my mystery-loving friends. All have become as smitten as I. When my wife went to London, her first priority was procuring a few of James' masterpieces that are not currently available in the United States. Each and every one is a delight. It's only a matter of time before James is widely appreciated for his genius. Get on the bus early for a good seat.

Andy Levine

Bearing Witness by Michael A. Kahn (2000)

Each time I read one of Michael Kahn's books featuring attorney Rachel Gold, I wonder why this excellent series seems to stay under the radar detector of many mystery readers and critics. Now six books long, the series combines humor, a cast of likable and unique regular characters of definite but unstereotyped Jewish ethnicity, sound legal procedure (as far as I can tell, anyway, but Kahn is, or was, himself a practicing lawyer), and well-paced, original plots. He also masters the difficult task of cross-gender writing, telling the stories in Rachel's first-person voice.

The first two books are set in Chicago, after which Rachel moves to St. Louis, a much less common setting for mysteries and one Kahn puts to good use:

"...what about this thing?" Rachel's good friend asks her about the Gateway Arch. "A humongous stainless-steel arch, planted on the banks of the Mississippi, stuffed with trainloads of yokels cruising up and down inside of it all day long. What the hell is this all about? Some weird Midwest shrine to Ray Kroc?"

The friend, Benny Goldberg, is a wonderful foil to the compassionate but more reserved Rachel: "He was fat and vulgar and loud and obnoxious. He was also brilliant and funny and thoughtful and savagely loyal. I loved him like the brother I never had..."

While the earlier books occasionally address serious matters such as spousal abuse, the humor always figures prominently. For those leery of the zany romp school of mystery humor, I hasten to add that the humor here is considerably more sophisticated and grows directly from the characters and their reactions to both specific situations and life in general. But *Bearing Witness*, while not without its humorous moments, takes on a big issue — I'll leave it at that, since to elaborate would be a spoiler, but suffice it to say that it's hard to imagine any reader unaffected by the revelations.

Rachel files a seemingly simple age discrimination lawsuit on behalf of Rose Alpert, a longtime friend of her mother's, which leads Rachel, Benny and Rose herself into a web of deceit and far worse. From a mystery standpoint, the story does leave a bit to be desired — there are a couple of very predictable events, some conversations that (in retrospect) unrealistically ignore certain obvious questions, a severe shortage of suspects, and a solution obvious to anyone who happens to speak a little German. But all of this is almost inconsequential in the face of a moving and compellingly told story. It's a cautionary tale that deserves a wide readership.

Bearing Witness works perfectly well as a standalone. If you've read the earlier books in the series, you'll see that this one ratchets everything up a notch. On the other hand, reading this one first takes nothing away from the first five. Read them all or read some; if you read just one, make it this one.

Maria Parker

The Red, White, and Blues by Rob Kantner (1993)

It might be the subject of a compelling night's debate, whether to include here the stylings of other creators of the traditional private eye, whether Jonathan Valin, Stephen Greenleaf or Arthur Lyons. They have all produced novels in similar styles, wonderfully written, concise, impressive — and virtually forgotten.

But Rob Kantner is the only one among this particular brotherhood to have been relegated to the "paperback original" venue, perhaps reflecting the publishers' lack of dedication to the cause of preserving the words in perpetuity. Yet, Kantner's Ben Perkins comes off as somewhat more human, more fully fleshed out than his fictional brothers. In fact, he may resemble no one so much as he does John D. MacDonald's legendary Travis McGee.

Perkins is blue-collar through and through, having been removed from Kentucky by parents looking to find employment in the automotive business of Detroit of the '50s. Perkins went to work on the line at Ford where he was elevated to membership in the union's inner circle, guarding the back of a senior union official suspected of pocketing union funds. Perkins kept his own counsel, spent time in prison for his silence and, upon release, used grateful union connections to get a job as superintendent at Norwegian Wood, a condominium complex that provides him a residence and enough employment to keep him honest while he's solving problems for friends and taking on other jobs that strike his fancy.

Following a nifty introduction and set-up, including Perkins breaking up a robbery at a high-brow social gathering, Carole, a lawyer, his sometime companion and the mother of his daughter, has an unusual request: to locate her client's child who's disappeared. Some obvious coincidences mar an otherwise intricately plotted novel, but they can't reduce the impact of Ben's means of fixing things: an all-out assault by an improvised commando force made up of an angry security guard, a disillusioned state trooper, a renegade newspaper reporter and weak-willed mid-level professor.

What sets Ben Perkins apart is his humanity — his self-awareness, his humility, his fallibility. Over the course of the series, from *The Back-Door Man* through this, his eighth and last, Ben develops and changes, particularly in his attitude toward the women in his life. Where he initially deals with women primarily as sex partners and drinking buddies — with the exception of Carole — he becomes a dedicated friend of the alcoholic Barb Paley, former inhabitant of Under New Management, the local dive; her presence had once been restricted to that of a boozy, bedable broad.

What we wouldn't give for a few more visits from Kantner and his tough guy, but there's no way to explain the thinking of publishers who seem to have no place for the traditional mystery or detective novels from the talented people who come up with great characters: flesh, blood, three-dimensional, fully alive. We miss you, Ben Perkins.

Kathy Phillips

Park Lane South, Queens by Mary Anne Kelly (1990)

When I began rereading this book to write this review, my first reaction was one of mild disappointment: my memories of it were so magical, I was expecting to be stunned with its power from the very first lines. Instead, it took a few pages till the characters and the neighborhood they live in took hold. But before long I was again overwhelmed by the combination of hilarity, tenderness, exhilaration, and melancholy nostalgia that this wonderful world evokes.

Mary Anne Kelly has that rare gift for creating richly vivid and wackily original characters, characters so engaging and authentic that they feel more familiar than friends by the story's end. Kelly skillfully uses a shifting narrative viewpoint that allows us to see the world from the point of view of each of the story's main characters: Claire Breslinsky, recently returned from years living in Europe and India after the death of her twin brother, rediscovering her old stomping grounds through the eyes of the camera that goes everywhere with her; her sisters Zinnie, the warm-hearted, down-to-earth cop, and Carmela, the flamboyant fashion-plate; her father Stan, who spends his retirement whittling perfect miniature artillery; her mother Mary, the matriarch who holds it all together; and, king of the hill and master of our hearts, the Mayor, the irrepressible bloodhound who is perhaps the most winning character of the bunch — and the most memorable dog in detective fiction.

Then a little boy is murdered, and Johnny Benedetto enters the scene: homicide detective, car fanatic, bit of a tear-about and, soon, smitten with the edgy Claire.

Interwoven with the delightful humor, which bubbles in every direction when two or more of this crazy crew get together, is a depth and breadth of vision, a psychological intensity, that make this at heart a very serious, and very moving, story. Every character has a hidden wound or inner torment that is touched by the crisis that unfolds as the community reels from the shock of the murder in their midst. Among mystery writers, perhaps only Reginald Hill can match Kelly's brilliant blending of comedy and tragedy.

Kelly wrote three other books about Claire: *Foxglove*, a much darker sequel with a twist that is probably unique in mystery series; *Keeper of the Mill*, a more meditative work; and *Jenny Rose*, a nonmystery that takes Claire back to Ireland to discover her (maternal) roots. All are absorbing, but none equals this intoxicating introduction to a bustling, ethnically diverse New York neighborhood, and the joys and sorrows of the offbeat and entertaining people (and animals) who live there.

Jill Hinckley

Iron Lake by William Kent Krueger (1998)

Lyrical. It's the best word I can find to describe Kent Krueger's style in the Cork O'Connor mysteries. His writing is like a beautiful song that washes over me and transports me into the world of the Ojibwe. He can take the eerie, the evil, and either the generous or the hellish side of people and describe it so beautifully, so profoundly, so eloquently that I am amazed by his talent.

Cork O'Connor is the former sheriff of the small town of Aurora, Minnesota. When a local judge is found splattered by a shotgun blast, suicide is the immediate ruling. The young boy who found the body is now missing, and his frantic mother pleads with Cork to find her son. Cork finds evidence contrary to popular opinion yet he fights to be heard by a town soured on his ability to investigate the facts.

Part Irish and part Anishanaabe Indian, Cork straddles the modern world and the ancient world of the tribe that lives in Aurora. He finds wisdom in the words of local medicine man Henry Meloux as well as in his law enforcement training. Caught in the void between marriage and divorce, Cork also struggles with the values of family and love and commitment and loyalty. Krueger has taken a simple man and made him complex with the issues of today's world. I was intrigued to see how Cork deals with the issues of his personal and professional life — trying to find balance between work and family. Complicating his life are the pulls from his children and estranged wife and his present girlfriend. The depth of these issues is what makes Cork so real, so life-like, so appealing.

Still there is a mystery here to be solved. The cold snow falling on Iron Lake may be hiding the clues Cork needs to find who murdered the town's judge and locate the missing boy. With the same careful attention to detail he has given his characters, Krueger weaves a tale that is believable, complex and engrossing. I was so riveted by this story that I forgot that I was sitting in my home in hot and humid Florida and grabbed for blankets and quilts. This is the mark of a writer with enormous ability to weave a captivating story.

Iron Lake has so far been followed by two more in this series — *Boundary Waters* and *Purgatory Ridge* — with contracts for two more. The character development of Cork O'Connor continues in depth along with that of his wife Jo, a lawyer for the Ojibwe tribe. The struggles of everyman are portrayed in Cork and his continuing search for his place in the world. Yet again, these subsequent books are mysteries with captivating tales of their own.

The issues Cork O'Connor deals with in *Iron Lake* are so fundamentally human and universal, that I am glad to know that Krueger will continue to guide his struggles in future books. I'm sure we'll be treated to superior mysteries in a magnificent land as well.

Sandie Herron

The Loud Adios by Ken Kuhlken (1991)

The term film noir refers to a style of filmmaking from the 1930s to the 1950s that involved techniques used in crime films. While the films were about visual style, certain expectations were developed about how film noir characters would behave. These characters are alienated from society, and compound their problems by making really bad choices. Ken Kuhlken has closed the circle by writing a brilliant homage to the original literary private eyes and to the characters of film noir. Tom Hickey, the featured player in *The Loud Adios*, is living a film noir life. Hickey already has failed as a musician and bandleader, LAPD cop, sailboat salesman and restaurant owner.

As this book opens in 1943, Hickey has just lost his wife and child to his former restaurant business partner. To survive, Hickey has opened an investigative agency with Leo Weiss. Then Hickey is drafted into the Army. While assigned to guard the Mexican border south of San Diego, Hickey is persuaded by a young soldier named Clifford Rose to cross into Tijuana to retrieve Clifford's sister, Wendy. She is known as La Rosa Blanca, and she is on display in a strip joint as the featured act. Clifford has not told Hickey the whole truth, something Hickey regrets when Wendy's connection to the Mexican mob, the government and a murder makes rescuing her a major challenge.

Confronting the corruption of a society in chaos, Hickey moves back and forth across the border as he tries to engineer Wendy's freedom. Despite gunplay that eliminates some of his allies, Hickey's quest is successful. Hickey's prediction that "maybe something in this business would stir his blues" proves true. All film noir characters make bad choices, and Hickey's are to fall in love with Wendy despite her mental disabilities, shortcomings that leave her believing Hickey is an angel sent from Heaven to rescue her. He is not. Hickey makes a worse choice when he is seduced by the gold held by the German agents. Weiss tries to warn Hickey, but the PI goes AWOL to create a small army of American and Mexican allies to enter Mexico once again to gain the gold.

This is a complex novel where every nuance has meaning and sometimes it is the blank spaces that tell the story. It is evocative of everything in both film noir and the classic private eye novel canon. Within its microcosm, it shows the futility of war and the sacrifices that all men make in battle. Bittersweet and romantic, this historical novel was selected as the winner of the Private Eye Writers of America Best First Novel Contest. It was followed by *The Venus Deal* (1993), a prequel to this story, and *The Angel Gang* (1994), the story of Wendy and Hickey's life together. The three novels comprise a trilogy that stands as some of the finest historical writing in the private eye field.

Gary Warren Niebuhr

The Debt to Pleasure by John Lanchester (1996)

For those who savor suspense along with their cooking tips, *The Debt to Pleasure* by John Lanchester will provide some simmering food for thought.

The story unfolds deliciously, like a slow-cooking bouillabaisse, which is one of the many tasty dishes that comes under scrutiny in this novel. Despite a wonderful cover, which would look terrific in a frame, and positive reviews, it was a handselling book right from the start and continues to be; it's not a book that appeals to everyone. However, it's a real gem for those who choose to delve into it. The writing is languid, literary even, with long-flowing sentences joining seemingly unrelated subjects as Tarquin Winot, a food connoisseur with an caustic wit, tells his tale in first person.

In France, Winot makes his way from village to town taking great pleasure in describing what pleases his eyes and his taste buds, occasionally throwing in a recipe or a preferred menu, and reminiscing about his brother, the servants and other details of his childhood. His passion is food and he likens a person's first restaurant experience to a first love. There are missives on everything from wine to aperitifs, art and words. He gets caught up in the description of food and expounds on such topics as "contemplated soups, theoretical soups, hypothetical, remembered and virtual soups." Recipes are sprinkled throughout and foods are often matched to seasons. For spring, he suggests food that is combative, up-tempo, and sanguinary. But all is not sanguine and the reader begins to feel a discomfort at an underlying, growing menace. The first mention of a death, of a former cook for the family, which had been thought a suicide or accident, deftly drops a hint of murder into the plot.

Winot's commentary is wickedly opinionated, with a gourmand's grasp of the seductions of food, and an underlying evil devoid of conscience. In short, he's an elegant, dapper sociopath.

The Debt to Pleasure is a beautifully written book for the senses and, not surprisingly, won the Whitbread First Novel Award. It's a book to be read, digested and reread several times over as each reading uncovers anew the subtle humor and layers of intrigue.

Lanchester was born in Hamburg, has lived in numerous cities around the world, and now lives in London. A book reviewer, restaurant reviewer and book editor, he's also had stories published in The New Yorker and Saturday Night.

Linda Wiken

The Nightrunners by Joe R. Lansdale (1987)

I became a fan of Joe R. Lansdale after reading *Savage Season*, the first Hap Collins/Leonard Pine novel, on a long flight. Aware of Lansdale's fine reputation as a horror writer, I was delighted by his masterful manipulation of the conventions of the caper novel as if he were a West Texas Richard Stark. I was smitten.

The Nightrunners was the first nonseries Lansdale novel that I read. It remains a favorite because it can be read as a crime novel or a supernatural horror story or both. All the essentials for a good horror story are present — premonitions, demons, ventriloquist's dummies, possession and Halloween. Yet these same elements can be rationally explained as manifestations of the psyches of the two prime characters.

Lansdale sketches a sensitive picture of protagonists Monty and Becky Jones. They leave Galveston to put their lives together at a lakeside cabin. Becky was raped by a feral pack of teenagers led by Clyde Edson, who was abandoned and arrested after the assault. Monty, a conscientious objector to the Vietnam War, feels tremendous guilt for not being present to protect his wife; Becky blames him for failing to save her. Becky experiences post-trauma nightmares, vividly dreaming that her rapist hanged himself in his cell. She cannot dismiss the dream as wish-fulfillment because she learns Edson committed suicide in that manner.

The suicide profoundly affects Brian Blackwood, the smartest of Clyde's cronies. In a philosophy combining Nietzsche and *Star Wars*, Brian believed that he and Clyde were supermen and two halves of a whole. After Clyde's death, the God of the Razor, beautifully described in all his grotesque glory, appears before Brian. The monstrous figure, speaking through a skeletal Clyde sitting on his knee, instructs Brian that he must kill Becky or be punished. Clyde possesses Brian to appease the God and ensure success.

If the God of the Razor is a figment of Brian's imagination, Lansdale has created a psychologically complex character similar to Norman Bates. Brian deludes himself to ease his guilt and grief over his role in his friend's death by speaking in Clyde's voice as if he were still alive inside him. If the novel is mere Grand Guignol, Brian simply becomes the boogeyman after this visitation. In the final section of the novel, Lansdale does not spare the frights or the gore. The novel races to its bloody climax on Halloween night where the Joneses make their stand against Brian and the remaining gang members.

While *The Nightrunners* cannot be favorably compared to later novels like *Freezer Burn* or the Edgar-winning *The Bottoms*, it is grand pulp fiction with all its pleasures and failings. The novel contains graphic sex and violence but these elements are shocking without being merely sensational. Despite many evocative images, the novel also has extremely melodramatic prose. But its raw power holds you tight.

Crime story or horror story? Columbine or *Halloween*? Lansdale's final description of the landscape by the cabin suggests that the God of the Razor exists. And consider that Lansdale subsequently wrote *Blood & Shadows*, a comic-book series for DC, where the God of the Razor, drawn precisely as described in the novel, is the central villain. Neither dispels the delicious ambiguity of *The Nightrunners*.

Joe Guglielmelli

Burn Season by John Lantigua (1989)

"Burn Season" is that time in agrarian societies when farmers burn their fields to clear away unharvested or dead crops in order to prepare for the next planting season. The land is blanketed in ash, which mixed with the high humidity preceding the rainy season, forms a haze that covers the countryside and drifts into the lowlands and the towns. During this time, insurgent groups undertake military operations against the established authority as the haze cloaks movement and negates superior air and fire power. If, however, the insurgents have not accomplished their goals when the rains arrive to wash away the protecting haze, they are left vulnerable to superior force.

The narrator of John Lantigua's *Burn Season*, Jack Lacey, is a New York expatriate who fought with the Sandinistas in 1979 and now owns the Tropical Club in San Jose, Costa Rica. He is feeling vulnerable. In the same manner and for the same reasons as his predecessor in popular culture, *Casablanca's* Rick, Lacey tries to remain neutral while war and conspiracy surround him. Unexpectedly, however, he finds himself in the middle when Topo, a small-time informant, is murdered outside of the Tropical Club after speaking with Lacey. Then two more customers of the Tropical Club are killed. Lacey has been around long enough to know that in Central America, the middle can be a very dangerous place. The Contras think he's a Sandinista spy, the Sandinistas want him back on their side, Costa Rican intelligence is unsure of his sympathies, and the Americans have their own plan for him.

Lantigua's plot is tight and still holds up after twelve years. As a freelance journalist, he reported from Honduras and Nicaragua and researched the plot's possibilities carefully. But what stands the test of memory best is Lantigua's spare style and his ability to convey a sense of time and place which is evident in the book's opening paragraphs:

It was the night they killed off Topo. That was a Wednesday, a slow night. A few tables were full with my regulars and, in the corner, a group of Nicaraguan exiles. The Nicaraguans always sat in that corner by themselves, talking over what they had to talk over.

It hadn't rained and the air was thick with heat and humidity. The ceiling fans cut through it slowly as if they were under water. On the sound system, Celia Cruz was singing about the

moon over Matanzas bay, and out on the dance floor a half
dozen couples drifted around, caught in the lazy currents of the
song.

Of course, some might think this reads like a winning entry
from Harry's Bar and American Grill Annual International
Imitation Hemingway Contest. If Hemingway was still around
in the 1980s, saw *Casablanca* again one evening and read the
next morning's newspaper, he might have written *Burn Season*.
                                                    Nancy-Stephanie Stone

Killing Suki Flood by Robert Leininger (1991)

Certainly it's a crime that *Killing Suki Flood*, a genuine treat
of a first novel by Robert Leininger, has not been reprinted in
American paperback. This suspense thriller is an ideal blend
and balance of character and dialog, setting and situation, plus
conflict and surprise. Savvy readers who investigate should be
able to find a copy in British paperback.

A perfect one-word opening sentence sets the stage and
foreshadows the action. Frank is fifty-four, a widower, a
friendly tank of a guy at 245 pounds, and until a few days ago
a long-haul trucker. He just wants to disappear into the De Baca
Mountains of New Mexico. Then, under a scorching sun and
blocking his road, he meets Suki. She's young, sexy, and
perched on top of a very hot red Trans-Am, waiting for someone
to come along and fix her flat. But it's not enough — the
engine's shot, and Frank isn't about to leave her to die in the
desert. It's a case of Man on the Run meets Girl on the Run.

The best suspense is often teasing in nature. Bit by bit we
learn more about Frank and Suki, and what has lead to their
encounter in the middle of nowhere. Frank has hijacked his own
last load, converting stolen ball bearings into $77,000 now
stashed in his truck. Cops are on his trail. Suki is fleeing for her

life from a sadistic, psychotic and terribly capable con man named Mink. Mink's button men, a brutish "Mutt and Jeff" pair named Mote and Jersey, are tracking Suki. They're supervised over the phone by Mink's right hand — his perverse and truly wicked stepmother Charlotte. The determined Mote and Jersey are already very close. Frank feels there's more behind this effort than a stolen muscle car, and he's right. It's not just what Suki took with her, but the farewell message to Mink she left behind — involving a needle and a bottle of India ink. The hunted become the hunters. Then the tables are turned again — and again? Frank and Suki's ordeal reaches a horrifying and unforgettable climax on the salt flats outside Reno.

Mink is a genuine monster, fresh and affecting. The novel is filled with sharp, short and colorful images. But the best metaphors are saved to describe Mink's evil. Frank, an everyman hero caught up in Suki's crazy conflict, is naturally reluctant to play "patty cake with a rabid dog."

There's some humor to leaven the tension. Jersey's phone manners will prompt a few sympathetic smiles. And just how did Frank lose his left index finger? It's a story that changes with anyone who raises an eyebrow, and may just get the reader laughing out loud. More than running gags, these are unifying threads.

Comparing Leininger to Elmore Leonard would be easy, but not quite correct. Every reader who discovers it will appreciate *Killing Suki Flood*. And nothing quite matches that moment of discovery — when a reader shouts a silent "Eureka!"

Jeff Hatfield

Death at La Fenice by Donna Leon (1992)

I still remember the excitement I felt when I saw Donna Leon's first novel, *Death at La Fenice*. I lived in Italy as a young adult and Leon immediately transported me back in time to the people and ambience of a country with which I remained enamored. That first Guido Brunetti mystery is still fresh and pertinent, and Leon's prose remains captivating. Most importantly, Leon knows her subject: the descriptions of Venice are so well done I still feel as though I am walking with Brunetti through the narrow calle and along the murky canale.

Each novel tends to focus on social values and mores of contemporary Italy and in my view Leon knows very well what hypocrisies may be found behind the walls of Venetian palazzi, as well as in the hearts of modern-day Italians. Through the course of ten novels she puts a laser-like focus on the environment, homosexuality, prostitution, mistresses, child abuse, the Church, stolen art, government corruption, fraud and murder.

Brunetti's interaction with witnesses, suspects, colleagues and family are enlivened with an inner dialog that is cynical, wry, witty, charming and hilarious by turns. He frequently gets the better of his immediate superior, Giuseppe Patta, a pompous, vain, and arrogant (albeit good-looking) Sicilian. "Even in a country of handsome men, Patta was shockingly handsome, with a chiseled Roman profile, wide-spaced and piercing eyes, and the body of an athlete, though he was well into his fifties. He preferred, when photographed for the papers, to be taken in left profile." Brunetti often makes a game of the discussions he and Patta have, silently betting what the Vice-Questore will do next. When Brunetti invariably guesses correctly, he deliberates over which flowers he should take home to his wife Paola, university professor and Henry James aficionado. Their children, Raffaele and Chiara, assist with commentary and observations on life in contemporary Venice. Although Raffi is attending high school in preparation for university, his disenchantment with education and the fate of the working class has left him in a state of not wishing to be either educated or a worker. And in this "Brunetti found the simplicity of Raffaele's reasoning to be absolutely jesuitical."

In this book Brunetti investigates the death of Maestro Helmut Wellauer, found dead in his dressing room at La Fenice just before the third act of *La Traviata*. Obviously an opera enthusiast, Leon sounds just the right note in describing the theater and those characters inhabiting that world, behind as well as in front of the curtain. Brunetti pounds the pavement much as any American detective; his willingness to review the evidence and continue to go over conversations with uncooperative witnesses so that he can ferret out the smallest detail is what makes him a great detective. Leon writes literate mysteries with plots. I think of her books as mini-vacations in Italy, and I hope you will, too.

Amy Proni

The Mystery of the Yellow Room (Le Mystere de la Chambre Jaune) by Gaston Leroux (1908)

Because of the books and stories I write and the anthologies I edit, it is always safely assumed that I am an unconditional fan of hardboiled writing. So let me confess to a guilty pleasure few suspect: I am a sucker for locked room mysteries. Sure, the dark streets and femmes fatales of crime fiction still please and attract me, but when it comes to tickling my intellect and my curiosity, nothing does it better than a tale of impossible murder and its meticulous reconstruction and explanation.

We usually equate this very specific niche of the mystery genre with John Dickson Carr (as himself and his alter ego Carter Dickson) or even Ellery Queen, but for me the best frisson afforded by these wondrous tales originated with Gaston Leroux, a sadly neglected French author principally remembered now for *The Phantom of the Opera*.

The Mystery of the Yellow Room was written in 1908 and, for me, has never been bettered. Joseph Rouletabille is a young, eager and endearingly naive journalist turned involuntary sleuth

106

who stumbles across a sinister murder by blunt instrument in the yellow room of the title. Of course, the room is hermetically sealed from the inside and every single suspect and protagonist has a perfect alibi. Rouletabille finds himself pitted against master detective, and soon to be his arch-enemy, Frederic Larsan. To complicate matters there is a curious web of family intrigues and secrets surrounding the case and all its protagonists, involving Rouletabille in more ways than one.

Pitted against the dark soul of the sinister if madly clever Frederic Larsan and the murky secrets of the Stangerson family, Rouletabille is soon at sea, in love, in search of love and more. Considering when the book was written, it remains remarkably modern, a veritable page-turner whose exploration of the dark side can still send shivers up my back. Further, there is a madly romantic aspect to the fragile young Rouletabille's quest that still touches me deeply inside. Naturally the solution to the dastardly crime turns out to be a twist within a tortuous twist for which even a Mensa reader might prove quite unprepared, but this sad resolution also adds strong elements of poignancy to its tale of a doomed family.

Leroux wrote a sequel a year later: *The Perfume of the Lady in Black*, in which the first case is revisited and which mischievously casts a very different light on its resolution and motivations, and adds a further tragic color to Rouletabille's quest for his own past. Together I have no qualm in calling the two novels a masterpiece. Leroux penned a handful of other Rouletabille adventures in later years, but none of the workmanlike adventures of the maturing hero ever recaptured the magic of his locked room mysteries.

Maxim Jakubowski

Warrant for X by Philip MacDonald (1938)
aka The Nursemaid Who Disappeared

Warrant for X may be the first popular detective novel in which the sleuth attempts to prevent a crime before it occurs, rather than solve a crime that has already happened. The set-up is classically simple: a young American playwright, Sheldon Garrett, accidentally overhears two people talking in a London tea shop. It seems that they are planning a kidnapping — a crime particularly abhorrent to Garrett because his sister's family was once so victimized. After being fobbed off by the police, he is introduced to Colonel Anthony Gethryn (Philip MacDonald's series sleuth) by an old friend, Avis Bellingham. With the assistance of the police, as well as Garrett, Bellingham and several "irregulars," Gethryn uses clues as mundane as a shopping list and a bus ticket to trace the criminals.

This is the apotheosis of a plot-driven, Golden Age mystery novel. The backgrounds and motivations of the main characters are streamlined, strictly the minimum required to move the story forward. The city of London, however, is described with a full freight of Chestertonian mood and atmosphere, so that the very houses are sinister and the tube stations are ominous. The pea-soup fog is as threatening as a man with a gun. Even Ye Willow-Pattern Tea Shoppe, although "brother to a hundred other Tea Shoppes," is unforgettably tainted as the scene of the conspiracy.

Although we generally enjoy the vantage of an omniscient narrator, we have particular empathy with Garrett, whose anguish increases as every lead to X either fizzles out or is blocked by the criminal's countermoves. The suspense builds continuously, as the stakes are raised by attempts on Garrett's life, a blackmail victim's suicide, and the murder of several potential witnesses. After an action-filled, clock-ticking denouement, we finally look into the blank eyes of X with a chill of loathing. X remains a dark mystery, however, with no attempt to provide psychological insight, criminal record, or sociological excuses for the villain (a refreshing change from the currently popular Hannibal Lecter school of psychotic voyeurism).

The enjoyment of *Warrant for X* lies in the thrill of the hunt — the extrapolation from a few lines of dialog and some apparently insignificant details to the identity and location of the criminals and their victims. Without a scene of the crime, DNA or other scientific techniques, Gethryn and his cohorts must rely on a mixture of common sense, intuition and ingenious ruses to trap a wily and ruthless antagonist.

Listed as a mystery-writing "cornerstone" by Ellery Queen, *Warrant for X* remained in print more or less continuously in the US until its most recent paperback reprint in 1983. Its UK title was *The Nursemaid Who Disappeared,* and it was filmed under that title in 1939. It was filmed again in 1956 (with significant alterations) as *23 Steps to Baker Street,* with Van Johnson and Vera Miles. MacDonald is the author of almost a dozen books in the Anthony Gethryn series, the best known of which is *The List of Adrian Messenger.*

Kate Derie

A Back Room in Somers Town by John Malcolm (1984)

Readers of mystery and detective novels have always appreciated getting a bit of arcane information along with their fiction. *A Back Room in Somers Town* by John Malcolm (Andrews) admirably fulfills this desire. It's the first of twelve crime intrigues featuring British art investment advisor, sleuth, and broken-nosed ex-rugger Tim Simpson.

Tim is just starting his career working for a cadet branch of the conservative White's Bank in London. His story opens with reminiscence, warning us of remembered "deaths and danger." The narrative that follows is flashback. A belated phone message from an agitated dealer, asking for an urgent meeting, sets Tim musing that: "urgency and oddness and doubt are anathema to the fine art trade." Marlowe, Poirot and Sharon McCone would echo that sentiment as applying to the private eye racket as well. He's stunned to discover the gallery owner stabbed to death, and only a couple of early twentieth-century British paintings missing, both of relatively little value — no motive for murder. Tim had viewed the pictures just a couple hours earlier, and only knows that a foreign client wanted to quietly sell them on consignment. The lesser of the two is a disturbing painting entitled "A Back Room in Somers Town" by little-known artist Mary Godwin. After surviving two vicious attacks, his suspicion that the key to this mystery lies with the sad little Godwin picture seems confirmed.

When the bank sends Tim to Sao Paulo to ferret out problems at its cosmetics business, he begins to think that the secret lies in Brazil. More than a few of his new contacts are hiding things from him. But what possible connection could perfume have to the painting? Before the perilous trail ends, Tim must literally travel full circle before coming up with answers.

The tidbits of British art history are fun, and the vivid contrasting of cool London with the warm Sao Paulo setting is interesting and very effective. Though there's a danger of too much detail and name-dropping with both, the international aspect is pleasingly informative, for the British did things that significantly changed the history of Brazil. And in addition to being a tale of two cities, *A Back Room in Somers Town* can be viewed as a contrasting tale of two women: Susan, the sophisticated art history expert at the Tate Gallery, and the sensual and earthy Paulista Nadia.

Tim Simpson is appealing — classy, but also masculine and tough, a protagonist who's at the center of a very credible and well-crafted plot. Parker's Spenser has boxing, Jerome Doolittle's PI Tom Bethany has free-style wrestling, while Heron Carvic's Emily Seeton practices yoga. Rugby is Tim's martial art. Strikes with shoulder, or head. An overarm purler to the neck is more effective than a sharp right cross to the button — if it lands first. A fresh angle that's kinda cool.

Jeff Hatfield

Mecca For Murder by Stephen Marlowe (1956)

In the 1950s with the arrival of mass circulation paperback originals came a change in the private detective story. Some private eyes went international. Their clients were governments and diplomats rather than private citizens. Usually, they kept their PI licenses and were counterspies rather than professional intelligence agents. Their mean streets were in Rome, Benares, Brasilia and Mecca as well as in New York and Washington, DC. Stephen Marlowe's Chester Drum is a counterspy whose cases are in exotic settings, involving international intrigue and political implications.

Drum is a widower, a WWII veteran and a former FBI agent with a law degree. Through his ex-in-laws, he has entry into the Washington power structure and society. When not on assignment, Drum can be found driving around DC in his blue and white De Soto convertible with various lovely ladies in the front seat. The opening paragraph of *Mecca For Murder*, while set in DC, hints of mean streets and dark alleys abroad for Chester Drum and a very different world from that of Philip Marlowe or Lew Archer:

The minaret had Washington's northwest skyline all to itself. Only the monument would dwarf it, but that was to my left and behind me as I made my way through the traffic on Embassy Row. If structures of stone could, the minaret and the mosque which it topped looked lonely. They were a long way from Saudi Arabia.

And Drum, of course, is a short way from trouble. Initially, his case seems like one for a traditional PI: a rich woman tries to break up the romance between her son and a dancer and stop them from eloping. After this fails, she hires someone to kill the girl, then belatedly realizes she needs the girl's testimony in a court case. Drum is hired to prevent the couple's departure and, after this fails, to safeguard her return. What makes things different is that the mother is a politically active lobbyist for Arab causes, the son is a colonel in the US Army, the girl is a Jordanian belly dancer, the trip is a Hajj to Mecca, and the assassin is a Muslim fundamentalist.

Marlowe mixes into the story a course on Arab culture and politics: the conflict between secular and religious authority in Saudi Arabia, the influence of the western oil companies in the Arab world, the arrogance and ignorance of the west and its diplomats, the emergence of pan-Arabism and its cautious flirtation with communism, and the intensifying Soviet-American rivalry. Interestingly, these topics still appear in spy stories 50 years later.

Most of the other eighteen Drum books stand the test of time equally well. Set in such places as Venezuela, Saudi Arabia, India, Germany, Brazil, Russia and Yugoslavia, they provide snapshots of the era. You'll not confuse these books with John le Carré's George Smiley books with their exploration of the personal cost of participation in intelligence. They are nevertheless fun reads.

Nancy-Stephanie Stone

Fugitive Colors by Margaret Maron (1995)

Margaret Maron is celebrated for her North Carolina mysteries starring Judge Deborah Knott, a Southern flower who handles attorneys and solves mysteries with ease. But Maron should be better known for her novels about Sigrid

Harald, a lieutenant on the New York police force, the focus of nine mysteries Maron wrote between 1982 and 1995. The relative obscurity of these mysteries is unjust: Harald is a complex, living character who grows to know herself and others throughout the course of the series that, unhappily, may end with *Fugitive Colors*.

The best part of reading the Harald novels is watching a romance develop between the chilly (or shy?) Harald and a world-renowned artist more than 30 years her senior, Oscar Nauman. The couple progresses from heated arguments during a lovely springtime in *One Coffee With* (1982), to prickly courtship during the summer in *The Right Jack* (1987), through developing trust during the autumn in *Baby Doll Games* (1988), to outright passion in the snow in *Corpus Christmas* (1989). So it is shocking to read in the very first chapter of *Fugitive Colors* that, come a new spring, Nauman is dead. Harald's grief is rendered so convincingly that it almost hurts to read of it. This rare picture of true mourning and the slow and incomplete ways in which a woman copes with it make this mystery one that deals with mortality in a tangible way that most mysteries never approach.

Harald is able to begin her journey back from despair mainly because Nauman has left her with an enormous responsibility: he has made her his heir and the executor of his estate, most especially including his artwork. Harald must immediately make decisions for a number of clamoring art dealers about whether a retrospective of Nauman's work should go forward. This setting gives Maron the opportunity to explore the art world, as she does in all the Sigrid Harald books; in one Harald book or another, one learns about how lithographs are made, listens in on a discussion of abstract art or is introduced to Gothic portraits. Here, in *Fugitive Colors*, one learns about managing galleries, showings and sales. It is through readying Nauman's work for the show, rather than through her police work, that Harald comes across a corpse; but the resulting return to her lieutenant's desk is what really starts to bring her to life once again.

The mystery itself is somewhat negligible in this book, as it is in many of Maron's mysteries, regardless of whether the heroine is Deborah Knott or Sigrid Harald. A number of characters have a motive to kill the rather unlikable victim, and clues are laid out in a clear line to the actual killer. But the process of solving the mystery does not matter here. What matters are the portraits Maron paints of men and women the reader has come to know over the course of the series, and particularly the silverpoint drawing of Sigrid Harald, delicate, intimate and intense.

Terry Weyna

Borderlines by Archer Mayor (1990)

Borderlines by Vermont author Archer Mayor is my favorite book in one of my favorite series. The main character, Vermont police Lieutenant Joe Gunther, is a likable everyman-type policeman whose hometown is gritty, working-class Brattleboro. In *Borderlines*, the second in the series, Joe makes a temporary break from his usual duties and his girlfriend, Gail, to take an out-of-town assignment. He volunteers to help the state attorney with an embezzlement case in the remote northeast corner of Vermont, known as the Northeast Kingdom. It's the poorest, most sparsely populated part of the state, near the Canadian border. With a stark, minimalist beauty all its own, the Kingdom has neither of the classic Vermont tourist draws — the Green Mountain ski resorts or the picture-perfect farmland.

Before reporting to his temporary boss, Joe stops at the small Kingdom town where he spent his boyhood summers with his Uncle Buster. At first, Buster and Joe's childhood pals seem older but otherwise unchanged by the years. Joe soon learns that almost nothing in town is as it was, thanks to the invasion of a cult-like group known as the Order. Although the cult members espouse antimaterialism and a back-to-nature philosophy, they have enough money to buy half the town's real estate and open a restaurant. Not long after Joe's arrival, an altercation breaks out between one of the cult leaders and a man who thinks his daughter has been kidnapped by the Order. Less than twenty-four hours later, a fire destroys the cult leader's house, killing him and his family.

As more murders ensue, the plot twists and ever-shifting focus keep the reader guessing to the end. The multilayered resolutions of the murders lead to a nail-biting final confrontation between Joe and the murderer. Played out at night in a foreboding granite quarry, it's one of the most suspenseful conclusions I've ever encountered. I also really enjoyed the wonderful character development and interaction, the fire fighting scenes, and the portrait of a struggling small Vermont town. This is the real Vermont, and it isn't always bucolic pastures filled with cows or pretty inns and village greens.

Mayor's series is one of my favorites for several reasons. One is his smooth and intelligent narration. Another is the setting, which is always as much a character as the Vermonters who inhabit it. The characters are terrific in their own right, though. Joe and the wonderful cast of supporting characters develop with each book. Joe and Gail's relationship, one of the series' strong points, continues to evolve. They survive some very dark times, yet remain believable and the relationship is portrayed with great sensitivity. Throughout it all, Joe never loses his best quality, his humanity. Whether you're a native New Englander or have never set foot here, don't miss this series!

Susan Ekholm

Boy's Life by Robert R. McCammon (1991)

Read the first four pages of *Boy's Life* and you won't be able to stop. Robert R. McCammon has written a truly wonderful tale that is destined to become a classic. So how can a book that has had more than 30 paperback printings be considered a lost gem? Well, booksellers have been handselling the book since it came out, but somehow it hasn't reached the mass audience that it deserves. Each chapter is a wonderful short story; strung together they make a magical novel. *Boy's Life* is the story of anyone who has struggled through the awkward years of adolescence.

In 1964, Cory Mackenson is twelve years old and lives in Zephyr, Alabama. Cory is becoming an adult while holding on to the magic of childhood. He fights monsters, soars through the clouds, sees ghosts, experiences loss and gets a glimpse of the man he will become. One day as Cory accompanies his father on his milk route they see a car shoot out of the woods and plunge into Saxon Lake. Cory's father jumps into the water to save the driver only to come face to face with evil — the driver is handcuffed to the steering wheel and a wire is cutting into his throat. As the car is sucked into the lake, the death grin of the driver is burned into his father's mind. Haunted by the unidentified man, Cory watches his father's agonizing struggle to preserve his sanity. Cory is determined to find the murderer hiding in Zephyr, fighting monsters — real and imaginary — to save his father.

One day during his summer vacation Cory has a dream. It is the last day of school and he is leaving his classroom for the last time that year. His teacher calls Cory over to her desk and says to him:

"No one ever grows up." Cory is confused, he knows everyone grows up. She continues, "They may look grown-up but it's a disguise. It's just the clay of time. Men and women are

still children deep in their hearts. They still would like to jump and play, but that heavy clay won't let them. They'd like to shake off every chain the world's put on them, take off their watches and neckties and Sunday shoes and return naked to the swimming hole, if just for one day... I have seen plenty of boys grow into men, Cory, and I want to say one word to you. Remember."

And Cory — or rather McCammon — does, and therein lies the wonder of the book. As you read you remember your own childhood, and try to find the magic you believed in back then, when you "ran naked to the swimming hole." You feel the years fall away and once again believe that anything is possible. Young adults will see the world differently — and better; adults will become wistful and wish they could start over. Recapture the magic — read *Boy's Life*.

Ken Hughes

The Murders of Mrs. Austin and Mrs. Beale by Jill McGown (1991)

Jill McGown is the author of eleven police procedurals featuring Detective Chief Inspector Lloyd (no first name, a la Morse) and his partner, Detective Inspector Judy Hill. The first book in the series is *A Perfect Match*; the most recent, *Scene of Crime*. McGown, who lives in Corby, England, has also written four nonseries mysteries and one suspense novel.

I must confess that I love British police procedurals. I am truly in my element when a customer asks for a recommendation and tells me that she (or he) likes English mysteries. I start with some big names just to get the lay of the land. "Have you read Colin Dexter? Elizabeth George?" Usually they have. I move on to authors not so well known: "How about John Harvey, Frances Fyfield, Deborah Crombie, Jill McGown?" Harvey, perhaps; Fyfield, maybe; Crombie, possibly; but McGown? Almost never do I find a customer who has read a book by Jill McGown. And although her work is frequently described as "exceptional" and "standout," she has yet to win any major mystery awards.

McGown's writing is notable for both its complex characters and its intricate plotting. Reviewers compare her to Christie and Sayers, but while McGown's plots are at least as engrossing as those of the Golden Age mystery writers, her books also include a contemporary emphasis on character development and relationships. Lloyd and Hill, partners off-duty as well as on, do not display the quirks of some of the other modern series detectives — no cats, no jazz, no crossword puzzles — but the realistic ups and downs of their personal association add an interesting dimension to the stories.

Throughout the series, McGown makes excellent use of various storytelling techniques. In *Murder...Now and Then*, the action effectively shifts between a current investigation and the events of a dozen years earlier, while in *Plots and Errors*, each chapter is presented as a scene in a play. Note well: while all of McGown's books are "smart" mysteries requiring close attention and thought, *Plots and Errors*, with its complex and convoluted story, is definitely not for the casual reader.

The Murders of Mrs. Austin and Mrs. Beale (fourth in the series) finds the recently promoted Inspector Hill off on a new assignment in nearby Malworth, while Lloyd copes with an overly enthusiastic replacement, Sergeant Mickey Drake. When Lloyd's team is called to a crime scene — the home of the murdered Leonora Austin — they find the telephone off the hook. The open line is traced to the residence of Rosemary Beale, who was also murdered — apparently during a phone call to Mrs. Austin. Since the Beale murder occurred on Judy Hill's new turf, Lloyd and Hill find themselves working together once again.

Although it isn't her case, Inspector Hill is convinced that the murder of Mrs. Austin (a casual friend of hers) is open-and-shut: the husband did it. Lloyd isn't so sure, and they're both hard-pressed to explain why the victims, who did not know each other, were on the telephone together at the time of the murders. The solution, when it comes, is surprising and memorable; an ending that makes you want to go right back to the beginning and start to read again.

Karen Spengler

Dead Letters by Sean McGrady (1992)

Postal Inspector Lieutenant Eamon Wearie feels an almost religious awe for the relics that accumulate at the United States Postal Service's Eastern Seaboard Mid-Regional Bulk Management Depot 349, a huge Baltimore warehouse that is the final resting place for thousands of misdirected envelopes, packages and bulk mail — dead letters. Returned engagement rings, mundane correspondence, unclaimed merchandise — it all speaks to him of people's lives and hopes and dreams. He likes to spend his lunch hour reading in the Unpublished Novelists' Hall of Fame, where manuscripts that were stuffed into flawed return envelopes by bored editors accumulate dust, while their authors wonder why they never heard back from the publisher.

Wearie is working on a case involving a pedophile and possible serial killer nicknamed the Executioner, who has been sending some very nasty pictures through the mail, when he runs across a stack of envelopes addressed simply to "James." He becomes obsessed with tracing the author of the love letters, a woman who signs her name Netti; at the same time he is following up slender leads in the Executioner case, which is itself a "dead letter" as far as the FBI and Wearie's bosses are concerned.

Wearie is something of a burnout case at this point in his life, divorced, drinking too much and looking for love in all the wrong places. He is not at all sure why he thinks finding Netti would provide a measure of redemption, but he perseveres. Although Wearie is a federal agent, he retains something of the bruised idealism of the best private eyes, a man who is not himself mean although he walks the mean passageways of Postal Depot 349.

Sean McGrady gives us an unforgettable picture of the Depot, an enormous, decrepit old building containing acres upon acres of the flotsam and jetsam of American life, all the way back to the days of the Pony Express. There is Sector 1040, where undeliverable tax refund checks stack up, and the North Pole, where full-time employees attempt to sort Santa's mail and forward the most needy and deserving letters to the appropriate charities. Drug-sniffing dogs and employees in golf carts wander the dimly-lit aisles between the tables, cartons, crates, vaults and piles of *stuff*.

Both Depot 349 and Eamon Wearie are great characters, emblematic of life in America at the end of the twentieth century. I have no idea if the USPS Dead Letters warehouse is anything like McGrady's portrayal, but if it isn't, it ought to be. Secondary characters such as Wearie's partner, ex-PI Bunko Ryan, and his lodger, the obsessive-compulsive Daniel P. Pinkus, are just as well-drawn and vivid. The dialog and settings, from Baltimore's Inner Harbor to the small towns of Pennsylvania, ring true. *Dead Letters* begins a worthwhile four-book series that continues with *Gloom of Night* (1993), *Sealed with a Kiss* (1995), and *Town Without a Zip* (1997), all paperback originals from Pocket Books.

Kate Derie

Beyond the Grave by Marcia Muller & Bill Pronzini (1986)

Marcia Muller is often called the mother of the modern female PI, having presented us with Sharon McCone some five years before either Sara Paretsky or Sue Grafton hit the scene. She is less well known for a trilogy featuring art security expert Joanna Stark and another trilogy in which young Elena Oliverez takes time from her job as museum director to sleuth. Bill Pronzini is best known for his Nameless PI series, and a number of fine standalone novels of dark suspense. However, he also wrote several Westerns, and in this tour-de-force joins his Western protagonist John Quincannon with Elena in a mystery that spans both centuries and cultures.

Born out of the history of California and the territorial wars between the United States and Mexico, *Beyond the Grave* is a fascinating multi-time mystery, beginning with the 1846 razing of a large Mexican-held homestead and continuing with the search for the family treasure over the next 140 years. Elena is captivated by a wedding coffer she finds at an auction, and is determined to obtain it for the museum. Taking her prize home, she examines it more closely and discovers a fragment of Quincannon's diary detailing his 1894 introduction to Don Felipe Velasquez, his search for the missing artifacts and his uncovering of a murderer. Elena becomes obsessed by Quincannon's story and the mystery he couldn't solve. Muller and Pronzini alternate their storytelling seamlessly but definitively, with Elena's present-day story told in the first person, Quincannon's historical mystery in the third. The sleuths both take time out to deal with personal problems ranging from unrequited lust to the illness of a close relative.

Much of the dual plot, from the personal angst of the major characters to Elena's late revelation of a victim and a murderer, are added frills that readers will find more or less interesting. It is the parallel between the historian's craft and the detective's that makes this story so compelling: tracking down the minutia lodged securely in someone's attic, in an uncatalogued library crate, in the memories of the elderly, in private journals, in otherwise overlooked corners of photographs and paintings. The idea that there are still very real mysteries to be discovered and solved in the most commonplace of personal papers is enough to make a wannabe sleuth out of anyone. It is difficult to say which story is the more exciting — Quincannon's search for the relics, or Elena's search for Quincannon's diary — and that may be because, while most of us know we will never solve a murder, we could all imagine ourselves stumbling across something of historical significance in Grandma's old steamer trunk.

Muller featured Elena in only one more short story — she has said that Elena "retired" from sleuthing — while Pronzini periodically revisited Quincannon in short stories over the next dozen years. Never again, of course, would the twain "meet," but their one adventure together is a must-not-miss.

Sue Feder

Blanche Cleans Up by Barbara Neely (1998)

Barbara Neely's series featuring Blanche White gives us a sassy, satirical, middle-aged African-American cleaning woman with a sharp eye for the pretenses of her wealthy employers and a strong need to protect the weak. *Blanche on the Lam* won both the Agatha Award and the Anthony Award, but my personal favorite is *Blanche Cleans Up.* In this one, she takes a hand when the drug- and sex-related problems of her elite Boston employers impinge on people she cares about.

What I like about Blanche is that she's willing to face life head-on. She has to. She's survived rape and pervasive racism (sometimes masquerading as patronizing benevolence). She's gone on the lam to escape a jail sentence for writing bad checks.

She's taken on the task of raising her niece and nephew, and deals with the problems raised by their developing maturity both unflinchingly and wisely.

Blanche views the panorama of contemporary life, especially race, class and status issues, with clear analytical intelligence. *Blanche Cleans Up* puts her in a position to observe and inwardly comment on a wide range of follies and frauds in the Boston Brahmin class. The old saying "No man is a hero to his valet" certainly applies to Blanche. She can spot a con job in the drawing room just as easily as on the street, and just may spit in the tea before she serves it. With the spiritual strength she gains from communing with the Ancestors and with the conviction that every experience can teach something, feisty and feminist Blanche doesn't take anything from anybody — except risks for the sake of the underdog or those weaker than she is.

She isn't easily fooled by others because she knows and accepts exactly who she is. Here's the opening paragraph of *Blanche Among the Talented Tenth*:

The size sixteen shorts slipped easily over her hips. Blanche gathered the excess material at her waist and admired the contrast between her deep black skin and the nearly colorless cloth... She used to buy larger clothes because she thought they made her look slimmer... Nowadays all she wanted was the strongest, most flexible body she could maintain. She was hoping to be using it for at least another forty-two years.

This emphasis on *use* permeates her outlook. At one point in *Blanche Cleans Up,* she muses that what she really wants is to use all her capacities for feeling, living, hoping, even suffering — she wants to be used up, not to die with part of herself unused.

Sometimes it seems that Blanche could have come straight out of *The Jeffersons*, but her humor is more than comic relief — it springs from a deep awareness of her own worth and of the common humanity that unites us all. Spending a few hours in

Blanche's company is a vividly life-affirming and highly educational experience.

Patricia Davis

The Dogs of Winter by Kem Nunn (1997)

As I reread *The Dogs of Winter* for this review I had to ask myself — is this really a mystery? True, it does feature several violent deaths, a kidnapping, drug trafficking and a murderer whose guilt isn't established until the final pages, but it is also so unlike the typical novel found in the mystery section as to suggest an altogether different realm. Although nonseries books regularly win the Edgar Award and climb the bestseller lists, ever since Sherlock Holmes the lion's share of recognition in the genre has gone to the authors who write numerous installments detailing the ongoing adventures of a single protagonist. As the book world becomes more and more ruthlessly businesslike, both chain retailers and conglomerate publishers have pushed the "genrefication" of literature in order to facilitate tidy marketing, and it seems to me that writers like Kem Nunn have been among their victims. If a book called *Crime and Punishment* or *The Secret Agent* came out today who can say what shelf the computer operator would route it to?

Not that it really matters — no matter where you stick it *The Dogs of Winter* is a masterpiece and I'm glad to have the opportunity to say it. The book begins with a drugged and dazed Jack Fletcher being awakened by a phone call. A former star surf photographer now on the cusp of middle age, Fletcher's devotion to the endless summer lifestyle has reduced him to shooting suburban weddings and popping pain pills when he is offered an improbable second chance. Drew Harmon, the reclusive legend of surfing, has insisted that Jack be the photographer when he reveals the secrets of the legendary Heart Attacks, "California's premier mysto wave, the last secret spot."

Jack's halting progress toward Heart Attacks in the company of Drew and a couple of callow modern surfers is interspersed with the stories of the residents of Sweet Home, the imprecisely named Indian village where Travis McCade of the Northern California Indian Development Council tries to keep the peace, and Kendra Harmon, Drew's wife, struggles to maintain her delicate mental equilibrium in the face of the growing certainty that her husband is guilty of murder.

Soon enough Jack's bumbling and Drew's arrogance cause the death of a young Indian boy, and his criminal kin, the "crankster gangsters," arrive to seek vengeance, first against Kendra and then against the surfers. The plot threads all meet in the classic American literary setting of the wilderness, "the end of things" where nature is both beautiful and deadly and human nature both heroic and vicious beyond measure, a place where both extinction and rebirth are possible.

Nunn's prose is beautiful, and he shows himself to be the rare master stylist who has the ability to create page turning suspense while still successfully engaging higher themes. When this book first came out I wrote that *The Dogs of Winter* is his triumph and our treasure, a mature, ambitious, highly readable masterpiece," and since I get the same chills up my spine at the conclusion every time I read it, I can only say that time has more than confirmed my opinion.

Jamie Agnew

The Pew Group by Anthony Oliver (1980)

None of the characters in *The Pew Group* is quite what outward appearances suggest. Doreen Corder would never have plotted to kill her tedious husband, Rupert. But when she made the spur-of-the-moment move — without even thinking about it, really — to extend her foot just enough to send him headlong down the stairs and into the great hereafter, she became, strictly speaking, a murderess. Who would ever have thought such a thing? Nobody, as it turned out. Not the coroner, not her neighbors, and certainly not her mother, the redoubtable Lizzie Thomas.

So while nobody suspects that a murder has taken place in the sleepy little village of Flaxfield, several of the inhabitants are very upset over the disappearance of the little Staffordshire pottery piece called the Pew Group. It's worth lots of money and lots of people want it. The piece turned up at Miss Hislop's bring-and-buy booth at the church jumble sale and several people became aware of its existence — but not before the unsuspecting traveling junk dealer Michael O'Shea bought the contents of the bring-and-buy booth to resell himself.

When the piece makes its way to the Doreen's antique shop she instinctively guesses that it might be a very good piece, but Doreen is more interested in the personal charms of Michael than a bereaved woman should be and doesn't mind the piece as carefully as she should. Eddie Cabert, a professional runner, spots it in the window of Corder's Antiques and notifies his wealthy American client. The vicar of St. Peter's in Flaxfield, the Reverend William Foley also knows exactly what the Pew Group is worth and he wants it as much as the wealthy American industrialist. He, unfortunately, doesn't have the same earthly resources at his disposal, but he is every bit as determined to have it.

It really is a good thing for everybody concerned that Lizzie Thomas has decided to move to Flaxfield to help Doreen adjust to her widowhood. (The fact that Doreen most emphatically does not want her mother's help is of no concern to Lizzie.) And the happy coincidence that brings former police inspector John Webber back to his boyhood home for his enforced retirement couldn't be more serendipitous. With the two of them investigating the disappearance of the Pew Group, the proceedings become, in the words of Newgate Callendar of The

New York Times Book Review, "A civilized, even absorbing piece of work... [Anthony Oliver is] a skillful and sensitive writer." He's also a very funny writer and a gifted story teller, and his humor runs the gamut from arch and witty to bawdy slapstick, some of it truly inspired.

Other novels by Oliver include *The Property of a Lady, The Elberg Collection* and *Cover Up*. His books are among the best crime fiction ever written.

Kathryn Kennison

Fast Company by Marco Page (1938)

I first noticed *Fast Company* as I pored through the riches at the Brandeis Book Sale several years ago. Picture the scene: all manner of folks young and old, rich and poor scrambling under the display tables looking for books. My kind of people! The outstanding cover art of *Fast Company* grabbed my eye. It was stark red and yellow, black and white with a bust of Dante, some rare books and a silhouette of a man running with a gun. I was really hooked with the lead that read: "Rare Books and Raw Murder Mix." My kind of book!

This is the story of book theft detectives told at a breakneck speed that recalls Nero Wolfe and Archie Goodwin. This book's partners in crime are Joel Glass and his sexy wife, Garda. Joel became a book sleuth when his rare book business failed due to the stock market crash. Joel's sleuthing originally seems harmless enough. It soon turns deadly, however, when an unscrupulous book dealer, Abe Selig, is murdered with a bust of Dante as the weapon, soon after a confrontation with Joel about some rare books. Selig had recently gained a hefty insurance reward after the theft of his book collection. He also stiffed several booksellers by stealing their customers. Joel calls him a louse and a smut peddler and is more than happy that Abe got his. But who killed him?

Written by Harry Kurnitz (1907-1968) under the pseudonym of Marco Page, *Fast Company* sparkles with fast action, great characters and witty dialog. Here are some examples:

"Where is the rest of the loot?"
"In the drawer," said Garda, rubbing herself ostentatiously.
"Two twenty dollar bills. I locked them in together in the hope that they would breed."

"Watch out, you'll spill my drink."
"I'll make you another. Do you love me in your nasty, cheap bookseller fashion?"
"To distraction, I never had a wife I loved so much."

Joel investigates Abe's murder and consults Julia Thorne, a knock-dead gorgeous aide to the late Mr. Selig. In a seduction scene worthy of Hollywood, Julia tells Joel that Abe was worse than Joel thought he was, dealing with stolen library property. Things ratchet up nicely as Mr. Terelli and the really bad gangsters show up, take pot shots at Joel and eventually kidnap him.

In a great scene Joel tells the gang how he outwitted them:

The seven of them came rushing at me, with guns and knives. I grabbed two of them — any two — knocked their heads together and threw them in the faces of the two others. That left three. West bid no trump, South passed and I doubled.

Joel eventually escapes, saves the books, deduces the murderer's identity and snuggles down for the night with Garda, ignoring the ringing telephone.

Fast Company is such a romp it is no wonder it became a movie in 1938 with Harry Kurnitz as the screenwriter. It starred Rosalind Russell and Melvyn Douglas as Garda and Joel. The movie is a delight. Two sequels followed, *Fast and Loose* and

Fast and Furious. Do yourself a favor and rent them if you can find them. But, read the book first! If you love the antics of Nick and Nora Charles, you'll love *Fast Company* with Joel and Garda.

Kathy Harig

The Apostrophe Thief by Barbara Paul (1993)

Sergeant Marian Larch is fed up with the New York Police Department. She's sick to death of her publicity-hungry captain, and has nothing but disdain for her partner, who has endangered her more than once with his slipshod work. She's planning to go out in a blaze of glory, resigning in such a way as to expose the venality all around her, when her friend, the star of a Broadway hit mysteriously called *The Apostrophe Thief*, calls her in a panic: the theater has been robbed.

And so begins this theater mystery crossed with a hardboiled New York police procedural. Marian Larch, the hero of seven of Barbara Paul's 22 extraordinarily diverse novels, is different from the run-of-the-mill modern female detective. She is not particularly likable; she has plenty of rough edges and a quick temper. These traits, combined with a sharp mind and an inability to suffer fools gladly, make it apparent why she would be anathema to anyone less competent than she.

Marian is temporarily transferred to another precinct to investigate the theater robbery — something of a surprise, given that the short-handedness of the police department usually means that such a crime would receive precious little attention. But some of the stolen items have considerable value, at least to collectors of theater memorabilia, so Marian finds herself busy during a time she expected to be doing little more than nursing her grievances. When the robbery case turns into a murder investigation, Marian is forced to reconsider everything, including her own future.

Paul has written all manner of genre fiction, from cozy mysteries starring Enrico Caruso to unusual science fiction novels. They are none of them standard fare. Perhaps most striking is Paul's ability to develop characters who are considerably more real than those one normally finds in genre fiction — like Marian Larch, a woman with a huge chip on her shoulder, one who is admirably professional yet who hasn't a clue how to handle disagreements with her coworkers, one who is quick and sharp when it comes to solving crimes but slow to realize what she wants for herself.

Paul's genius with character extends to setting; here, the theater itself has life and breath. Paul obviously has considerable familiarity with the world on the other side of the footlights, and she easily conveys the excitement of a play as it develops over a run, the thrill of seeing actors put themselves so completely into their characters that they surprise themselves with what they do on stage, and even, ultimately, the ways in which theater is just a business like any other. She develops the world of the theater collector — that netherworld where the hairbrush of a star is worth hundreds of dollars — into a fascinating subculture that one can almost begin to understand.

Paul hasn't written a Marian Larch mystery for four years now. It's a shame: Marian is one of the most interesting characters to grace the page in many a year.

Terry Weyna

The Big Blowdown by George P. Pelecanos (1996)

Mystery Loves Company had been in business several months when we received a letter from a new author asking if we would do a signing for him. We contacted George Pelecanos and worked out the details. In fact I think my exact words were "if you'll take a chance on us we will take a chance on you." Several days later the book arrived. It was titled *A Firing*

Offense. I read it immediately, and found it a well-written book with wonderful character development. The main character, Nick Stefanos, is an appliance salesman in Washington, DC — not your usual DC protagonist. Every year since that time George has been back to sign with each new book, better than the one before.

The fifth book in the series, *The Big Blowdown*, takes us back in time to Washington at the end of World War II. Peter Karas and Joey Recevo are two kids from the rougher side of Washington who have returned from the war to find that the easiest work they can get is less than honest. They take a job acting as muscle for one of the local bosses. Pete gets into trouble when the head of the gang learns that he has been soft on some of his fellow countrymen. He is attacked and severely injured by some of the other gang members. His recovery is a slow process, leaving him with a painful limp.

Pete then gets a job working at Nick Stefanos' grill as a prep cook. Things seem to be going well until Nick tells Pete that there is a mob boss who wants to make all of the small businesses pay protection money. Pete realizes that this is his former gang, and he devises a plan which should ensure that no harm will come to Nick or the business.

Most people think of Washington as the capital of the United States with the White House, Congress and all the monuments — the hub of political power. They aren't aware of the parts of the city that Pelecanos writes about. His attention to detail is amazing and his small bits of humor add to the story. His books are dark, gritty, hardboiled, and some of the best writing around. When you finish one of his books you feel exhausted from the ride you have just taken. I have a friend who read one of his books and said "I hated the subject matter but the writing was so good I couldn't put it down."

Paige Rose

The Butcher's Boy by Thomas Perry (1982)

Machinist Al Veasy in Ventura, California has a major bone to pick with his union officials. They've invested heavily in an outfit called Fieldston Growth Enterprises, which looks great on paper but is tanking performance-wise. The pension fund is dwindling at an alarming rate. Al doesn't have long to worry about investment irregularities, however. After voicing his concerns at the local's meeting, he starts his truck in the parking lot and is blown to kingdom come.

Department of Justice data analyst Elizabeth Waring in Washington reads computerized obituaries for a living, tracking suspicious deaths as the possible handiwork of a hit man. She tags Veasy's death as questionable and launches a tentative investigation. She quickly rules out suicide, concentrating on the union meeting. Heading to California with an FBI explosives expert, Waring is rerouted to Denver. A senior statesman with a controversial agenda is dead in his hotel room, the victim of a poisoning.

Waring is right on the money. The activities of the good guys are chronicled alongside the progress of the hit man, a nameless assassin known only as "the Butcher's Boy," protégé of underworld legend Eddie Mastrewski. Thus far he's lived up to expectations with clean kills and no trace of his involvement. His is a solitary existence, free of romantic or familial entanglements. Success in this deadly business requires he be a human chameleon, a nondescript figure adept at blending into the crowd. But his luck takes a turn for the worse on the Denver job. Muggers leave him with some very memorable injuries. The Butcher's Boy carries out his assignment and heads to Las Vegas. Suddenly he's the center of attention and very uncomfortable.

This is Thomas Perry's first book, for which he (deservedly) won the Edgar Award for Best First Novel in 1983. The reader walks a suspenseful tightrope between the prey and predator, not always sure which is which. Waring's frustration with her first experience of bureaucratic hurdles is almost palpable. So is the loneliness and unhappiness of the hit man. Plotting here is intricate, as the good guys isolate their target's slayings while the bad guy sets the Mafia bosses at each other's throats.

Perry followed up his first effort with another complex caper tale, *Metzger's Dog*. He brought back the Butcher's Boy ten years later in *Sleeping Dogs*. Most readers today know him for the popular Jane Whitefield series. I'd forgotten what a really powerful debut this book was. And the book's opening murder reminded me that there's nothing new under the sun.

Beth Fedyn

The Seventh Sinner by Elizabeth Peters (1972)

Beneath its contemporary setting and thoroughly modern mores, *The Seventh Sinner* is a sort of hip tribute to the Golden Age mystery novel.

The story begins in Rome in the early 1970s with "The Seven Sinners," as they call themselves, who are all students at the prestigious Institute of Art and Archaeology. On one of the group's expeditions around Rome, Jean Stuttman discovers a fellow student dying, his throat slashed. The death is ruled a suicide but soon one potentially lethal "accident" after another starts to plague Jean.

Viewing all this with growing unease is a new acquaintance of the group, Jacqueline Kirby, a visiting American librarian mixing business and pleasure in Rome.

It's this character that I find to be a particularly amusing allusion to the Golden Age. Jacqueline is eccentric, she bursts into song unexpectedly, constantly misplaces her glasses — usually on the top of her head — and carries a purse large enough to house a pony. She is opinionated, autocratic, perceptive, logical and formidably intelligent. She doesn't suffer fools gladly or at all for that matter. In short, Jacqueline Kirby is a Great Detective.

It is an absolute pleasure to watch Peters ring the changes on other hoary old conventions of the genre. The murder victim's cryptic dying message is worthy of Ellery Queen, for example, although it's typical of Peters' erudite flair that the message is scrawled in the first century dust of a temple to Mithra.

The rest of the cluing is equally eclectic although solidly within the bounds of fair play. Who else but Peters could conceal clues in the iconography of early Christian art, French invective, Roman mathematics, modern fashion and the lives of the saints? Even a withering comment about "over-educated" youngsters turns out to be a pointer for the alert reader.

Of course, there is also the scene in which the killer is confronted and forced to confess, as well as the detective's grand summation at the end of the novel.

Jacqueline may be a Great Detective but she's no stereotype. She is a fortyish mother of two grown children who viewed their departure from home with fond relief. She's a successful professional — can you name other Great Detectives with solid careers? — and a woman making her own way in the world. She is also something of a siren when she chooses and has a particularly satisfying romantic triumph in the last chapter.

So how does the modern woman come to detection? Amusingly, Peters advocates motherhood as good training. And, as Jacqueline demonstrates, guile and strategy are career assets. (Jacqueline herself thinks she arrived at detecting by habit. "In both my professional capacities I've been laying down the law to the young for twenty years.")

The pioneering female PI has received great fanfare, but who has ever applauded her more cerebral sister? Here's a toast to Jacqueline Kirby, the first liberated Great Detective!

Kate Stine

Down in the Valley by David M. Pierce (1989)

In 1989, I had been reading mysteries for years. I had always been drawn to books with strong characters, clever dialog and something that would set the story apart from all the others I had read. *Down in the Valley*, the first in a short series by David M. Pierce, is such a story. There are only seven books in the series, not all of them available in paperback, but they are worth scouting around for in order to meet V. (for Victor) Daniel, private investigator.

Vic Daniel is a different sort of detective. He is not just tall, he is very tall (6'7-1/4"). He lives in California like lots of other private eyes, but in the San Fernando Valley. Vic is a loner in some ways but he has a fairly steady girlfriend and a family that he's close to. I remember reading about his mother who has Alzheimer's and thinking "Now you don't read about many detectives and their moms, much less a detective who arranges his life around her care."

The supporting characters are just as unexpected. My favorite is Sara, a teenager with dyed green hair, multiple ear piercings and plenty of attitude. Sara considers herself a poet, a misunderstood one, of course. She comes to Vic asking him to find her birth mother and ends up helping him on a case. He finds that she comes in very useful and is able to go places a huge, male private eye might not. The "reports" she submits, including a list of her expenses, are a treat. Sara becomes a continuing character and the interactions between the two of them remain favorite parts of the stories.

The mystery? Oh yes, there is a problem for Vic to solve. He is hired by the vice principal of the local high school to figure out where students are getting their drugs and why the school seems unable to handle the situation. Using a nondisguise, great interview techniques and some highly illegal methods, Vic is able to solve the case to everyone's satisfaction. Sara is quite pleased at her small but important role in the proceedings. Her expenses? Two phone calls at 10¢ apiece (remember, it was 1989) and two cokes at $1.20.

Aside from wrapping up the "big case," Vic is also able to survive a fire bombing, help Sara locate her birth mother, attend a funeral, find out who is stealing from the bowling alley, go on a date and take care of his mother. What a guy!

Jean May

Common or Garden Crime by Sheila Pim (1945)

We first learned of Sheila Pim from Jacques Barzun and Wendell Hertig Taylor in their readers' guide, *A Catalogue of Crime*, in which they praised *A Hive of Suspects*, the only one of her four mysteries to be published in the US. This is the only reference to Pim we've been able to find, other than the glowing contemporary reviews that greeted each book. Her humorous and affectionate portraits of small-town Irish life led critics to proclaim her the Angela Thirkell of Ireland. Why she is so little-known today is something we can only speculate about.

Her first mystery, *Common or Garden Crime*, is set in 1943 in Clonmeen, a small town on the outskirts of Dublin, where sensible, middle-aged, Anglo-Irish Lucy Bex keeps house for her widowed brother Linnaeus and is a surrogate mother to his son Ivor, an RAF officer who is home on leave. His presence brings the war in Europe a little closer for Clonmeen's residents, who observe Irish neutrality and are far more interested in who is stealing a neighbor's fig crop than in what is happening on the Eastern Front.

What really captures their attention, however, is the murder of Lady Madeleine Osmund with monkshood harvested from Lucy's own garden. The Irish Guard is called in to investigate, and while Lucy respects their intelligence and the resources at their disposal, she also realizes that her intimate knowledge of her neighbors coupled with her extensive horticultural expertise puts her in a unique position to solve the crime herself. So she begins a parallel but nonadversarial investigation of her own, sharing information with the police when appropriate, and never failing to attend to the needs of family, friends and garden even as she searches out the murderer.

The book is one of the first mysteries to fully integrate a gardening background into the story. The horticultural details are no gimmick but are pivotal to the plot and govern the characters' daily lives. Gardening is not just a hobby for Lucy Bex but a necessary (and rewarding) way of life. The kitchen garden is a constant source of fruits and vegetables for the table, especially welcome during wartime shortages, and the flower garden is the basis for such absorbing social diversions as the annual flower show. Like most of her friends and neighbors, Lucy Bex knows the Latin names for all the plants in her garden, appreciates the value of a nicely composting manure heap, and is familiar with the best ways of putting food by. Throughout the story she is nearly as preoccupied with bottling her tomato harvest as she is with uncovering the murderer.

In the end, Lucy and the police solve the crime simultaneously. She also sees her nephew paired off with a suitable young woman, learns who has been purloining the Nichol-Jervises' green figs, and finishes putting up her tomatoes, all with her usual good humor and lack of fuss. There is an equal lack of fuss in the narrative, which gleams with quiet wit and sharply observed details of the villagers' daily lives. A mystery of manners to rival any by Pim's English contemporaries, it's a novel to savor both in the reading and the recollection.

Tom & Enid Schantz

Dover and the Unkindest Cut of All by Joyce Porter (1967)

Here is one of the funniest authors you have probably never heard of. Before M.C. Beaton, Dorothy Cannell and Lauren Henderson, another British crime writer, Joyce Porter, was writing wildly amusing whodunits starring her overweight, bilious and incompetent sleuth, Scotland Yard Detective Chief Inspector Wilfred Dover. Dover doesn't so much solve a crime as stumble upon the solution, that is, when he is awake and sober enough to stumble.

In the fourth Dover novel, *Dover and the Unkindest Cut of All*, the chief inspector and his wife are on their way to Filbury-on-Sea for their annual fortnight's holiday when, through the pelting rain, Mrs. Dover witnesses a young man jumping from a cliff to his death. Never one to intentionally get involved in that foul four-letter word — "W-O-R-K" — Dover is nonetheless forced by the local constabulary to postpone his vacation until the reason behind the man's suicide is discovered. In this mission, the chief inspector is aided by his long-suffering, handsome subordinate, Sergeant MacGregor, a man who is used to his boss's mood swings, memory loss, poor eating habits, fifteen-hour naps and chronic dyspepsia.

Through the course of the investigation, Dover meets several residents of the seaside resort town of Wallerton — a septuagenarian movie siren; a lady veterinarian with a boxer's face; a nearsighted, exhibitionist cab driver — none of whom would particularly miss Dover should he return to London and let them sort out their own mess. In the end, our intrepid sleuth has had his fill of Wallerton and decides to "solve their flipping case for them and they could put that on their needles and knit it." And if this means hanging MacGregor out as bait for the cunning killers, then so be it; where the abuse and humiliation of his minion is concerned, Dover is more than willing to go beyond the call of duty. When you find out what's behind the mysterious disappearances and deaths in town, you should laugh yourself silly.

As do all of Porter's deliciously humorous Dover novels, *Dover and the Unkindest Cut of All* contains several giggles on each and every page, humor that's as wicked as it is side-splitting. I highly recommend all in the series, but those worthy of exceptional mention include *Dover One* (the series debut, which includes one of the truly unique motives for murder in all mystery fiction), *It's Murder with Dover* (where suspects seem to be popping up left and right, nearly prompting Dover to pick one at random and be done with it), and *Dover Strikes Again* (someone's out to kill Dover; but even worse: the town's only hotel is unlicensed, and Dover must go without his booze).

David Thompson

The Wailing Frail by Richard S. Prather (1956)

Richard S. Prather, the creator of private eye Shell Scott, is funny. This sense of humor, found in the 34 Shell Scott novels published between 1950 and 1987, distinguishes Prather from the pack of paperback writers that exploded into print after the enormous success of Mickey Spillane. It is why the Shell Scott novels remain entertaining.

The charm of the Prather novels can be traced to his protagonist. Shell Scott is neither the gritty avenger like Mike Hammer nor the brooding loner like Philip Marlowe. The pop culture analogy to Scott would be Dean Martin's stage persona — drink in one hand, cigarette in the other, surrounded by beautiful girls but completely serious about his work. Scott, with his inch-long white crew cut, tools around Hollywood in his Cadillac interviewing and wooing every pretty woman in an investigation. But when he needs to be tough, he can shoot, fight and kill like Hammer.

The opening scene of *The Wailing Frail*, a novel

representative of Prather at the height of his creativity and popularity, displays his humor. It is Little Red Riding Hood by way of Gypsy Rose Lee. A legislative committee investigating political corruption hires Scott to interview witnesses who wrote with allegations of wrongdoing. Scott rings the doorbell at the day's last address to find a beautiful redhead "nude as a noodle" answering the door and looking for her grandma. Robed, the redhead explains that Grandma likes to ring the doorbell and then hide in the nearby bushes. Once Grandma is located, Scott learns that crackpot Grandma wrote the letter to the committee.

Scott's next witness promises to expose a "Mr. Big" orchestrating wide-ranging corruption through blackmail and bribery. He is shot next to Scott in a nightclub before revealing anything. Scott hunts for this criminal mastermind and stumbles across bodies — some dead and bleeding, some curvy and hot-blooded.

The novel's central scene is pure bedroom farce. Waiting for a crucial telephone call, Scott arranges for a date with one of the main female characters: Paula, the committee's administrator; Toddy, whose institutionalized father could be Scott's key witness; and Satin, a nightclub dancer who believes in spirits. While only Satin accepts Scott's invitation to his apartment, after some shenanigans, all three eventually arrive and confront each other. Especially a soaking wet Satin clad in just a towel. Only murder gets Scott off the hook.

Scott even cracks the case in comic style. With fluorescent makeup and ultraviolet light, he convinces Satin that he has been murdered. She then provides him the needed clue to Mr. Big's identity. The novel comes full circle with Scott, after the final shoot-out, optimistically answering his apartment door to greet the beautiful woman on the other side.

Arguing that Prather is sexist is not totally justified. The *Frail* women are portrayed as uniquely intelligent. Even the flaky Satin cogently articulates her attitude towards life. ("I'm an independent woman and they're going to think what they want anyway.") And the novels are not misogynistic because Scott honestly enjoys the company of women. Prather's attitude towards women may be dated but no more so than the attitude in the acclaimed Travis McGee novels of John D. MacDonald. Which, it happens, were written to replace the Shell Scott novels when Prather left Fawcett.

Joe Guglielmelli

Shackles by Bill Pronzini (1988)

Bill Pronzini's *Shackles* almost defies description — a run of the mill private eye story? No, not by a long shot. Okay, the main character is "Nameless," Bill's lone wolf, San Francisco-based, ex-cop-turned-private-investigator. But there all similarity to the private eye genre ends.

At the beginning, Nameless is chloroformed and taken captive by a ski-masked, unknown assailant. When he awakens, he's in a car, handcuffed and covered with a blanket in the back seat. He manages to push the blanket off enough to determine he's being taken to a remote section of the High Sierra. He is chloroformed a second time and when he next awakens he discovers a band of steel, five inches wide, padlocked tight around his ankle. The steel band has a metal loop welded to a thick chain about twelve feet long which in turn is attached to a steel ring bolted into the wall of a cabin. The cabin has one window.

He's on a canvas cot and his mind recoils as he sees the room only has about 50 feet of cleared space. There are meager supplies of food, reading and writing materials, and a few items for warmth. A small cubicle holds a lavatory and a sink. He can see out of the one window in the room and see that he's in the woods and patches of snow are all around. Even if he breaks the window open, he's still shackled and can't get away.

Late in the afternoon, his captor returns wearing a ski mask. He wants Nameless to remember him and what was done to him. He says he won't kill Nameless, but there are only thirteen weeks of food after which Nameless will starve. Once Nameless escapes, his search for his captor takes him to a variety of Northern California locales and eventually leads him back to the scene of his ordeal.

Almost half of the book is interior dialog and journal-style notes that could have easily turned boring or clichéd. Not with Pronzini, as he stretches himself and the private eye story. You remain fascinated and intrigued as to what Nameless will do next. Will he survive and how? Will he discover who shackled him and get his revenge?

For several years in Mysteries & More bookstore, we offered a money-back guarantee to any customer who bought this book. We never had a single return, and we sold over four hundred copies. This book was an Edgar nominee and in our opinion deserved to win. Unfortunately we didn't have a vote.

Pronzini is a master craftsman and a master story-teller and the Nameless series has never once failed to entertain nor has the series grown stale. We are sorry to hear that *Bleeders*, just published by Carroll & Graf, will be the final episode of the series. Bill also writes superb thrillers; *A Wasteland of Strangers* also received many nominations. In that story, Bill did something that few writers are capable of doing — he wrote the book in seventeen different viewpoints and not once was the story in the main character's point of view.

Pronzini once said that writing is not what he does, a writer is what he is — so I know we'll continue to have wonderful books from him.

Jan Grape

I Was Dora Suarez by Derek Raymond (1990)

A necessary disclosure: Robin Cook, who wrote as Derek Raymond, was not only a close friend of mine but I am now the executor for his estate. I hadn't read his books when I first came across him at the Mystfest film festival in Cattolica, Italy in the late 1980s. He was a cult author all across Europe but most of his books were then out of print in English. He was even more colorful than James Ellroy (also present), lurking cheerfully around the local bars near the sea front, a glass in hand, dispensing sagacious advice and outrageous stories from his murky past, a cadaveric presence never seen without his fading black beret even at the height of the Adriatic midday sun. Frankly, at first I didn't quite know what to make of him: poseur, eccentric or con artist? But I swooped on his books when I returned to London and my breath was taken away: this was a crime writer like no other, a human being touched by the hand of genius.

The following year, Robin returned to London from a decade-long European exile and, out of friendship and admiration, I became his agent. I read the manuscript of his fourth Factory novel, *I Was Dora Suarez,* on a flight to New York. I never saw the hours go by. A few weeks later I began the process of extricating Robin from his past options and contracts and getting him back into print, notwithstanding a major British publisher turning the book down because it had made him physically sick!

The Factory series, begun in 1984 with *He Died With His Eyes Open*, features a nameless cop based in a police station in London's Poland Street. His life is a mess and he is always the one landed with the cases no one else is much bothered about: the deaths of the downtrodden, the tramps, the whores, the forgotten flotsam of contemporary society. *Dora Suarez* begins with the excruciatingly slow and systematic description of the murder of two women and is one of the most savage, if realistic, pieces of writing I have come across. This is what real-life mindless, senseless violence is like and the prose never shies from the horror; truly a journey to the end of the night. But the nameless cop who confronts this sordid case just cannot shake the vision of Dora's face from his mind and makes it his sacred mission to avenge her death and confront the monster responsible. Dora, a young woman who dabbled in drugs and prostitution, has no mourners and died quite alone: he will become her angel of vengeance.

You don't read Robin's books for their plot, but for the intensity of the feelings, for the sacred fervor and sheer depth of compassion and empathy for the disadvantaged. Violent they may be, but they are also some of the most moral crime novels I have come across — even biblical in their wrath.

Before his early death in 1994, Robin wrote two more novels, neither of which found an American publisher. In Europe his books still outsell many of the biggest names in the field. Film-makers still hover like vultures around his legacy and a major reappreciation is seriously overdue. His time will surely come and the dead souls he wrote about will be rescued at long last.

Maxim Jakubowski

Bird Dog by Philip Reed (1997)

According to Harold Dodge, the beer in Chile is so good, you can even drink it warm. Is it true? I don't know, but part of me believes him. Can I find out? I suppose so, but you see, Harold Dodge isn't even a real person.

Harold is the main character of Phil Reed's first novel about a former "bird dog," a person who brings potential buyers into a car dealership. He's written a book called *How to Buy a Cream Puff*, so when Aerodyne co-worker Marianne Perado gets caught in a bad deal for a new Matsura in trade for her Ford

Escort, she seeks out his help. Harold accompanies Marianne to Joe Covo's car dealership. They meet with Vito, the salesman, and attempt to unwind the deal. Vito reveals that her car has already been sold, but Marianne perseveres, setting off a complex chain of events that gather speed like a car with no brakes.

Accidents, guns, dead bodies and mistaken identities follow. As complicated as this story becomes, I never lost track of which character was which. Nor did I have to make myself a "cheat sheet" of what happened when. I found myself able to follow the storyline with no hesitation or confusion. This is very important in a mystery when the reader is following carefully organized clues placed by the writer and timed just so to reveal the whodunit of the entire story. Reed does this splendidly.

Even the most minor character has dimension and depth. The hit man flown in from out of town to secure the missing black book brings his own story that gives meaning and understanding to how he could beat another man to near death and live with his own conscience. Joe Covo's wife wants to be involved in her husband's life so she reads books on cars and eventually knows more about engines than the car salesman does. These seemingly tiny details round out the personalities of each person in the book so that I felt as if I had some insight into who they were and what they might feel or do as the story progressed. I need to care about the characters, good or bad, to keep my interest going and keep me flipping pages.

I read a mystery to be entertained and to try to make sense out of seemingly senseless acts, or I try to organize clues into a pattern to solve a crime. I don't want this to be easy nor do I want it to be so very difficult so as to frustrate me. Reed has found the perfect balance in his writing that both tantalizes and taunts me.

Harold Dodge has appeared in only two books thus far: *Bird Dog* and *Low Rider*. However, Reed had gone on to write a novel entitled *Marquis de Fraud* about the world of horse racing which is as enticing as *Bird Dog*. I hope the future brings many more books from Reed, an author who balances the elements of mystery flawlessly.

Sandie Herron

The Line-Up by Helen Reilly (1934)

An early installment in Inspector Christopher McKee's career, this juicy detective novel has all the right Golden Age ingredients: society people, cantankerous head-of-the-family, gorgeous money-hungry wife, old family secrets, shifty-eyed male secretary, hunky young family physician, possible familial insanity, plus a likable policeman as the protagonist, and just for garnish, a charming young nurse a la Miss Pinkerton! Then there's murder by poison, another murder by poison, forgery, check kiting, dope smuggling, mobsters, a shooting at a country house, tons of up-to-date 1930s police procedure, and a denouement in the inspector's charming studio apartment showcasing a peculiar globe-trotting spinster with a very long memory. Who could wish for more?

In the hands of a hack this would be laughable, but in the talented hands of Helen Reilly the effect is that of solid, comfortable storytelling, a treat to be relished. Although this entry is the fourth "case" in Inspector McKee's long career, my Crime Club copy from 1934 persists in blurbing it as "his second case," with "McKee of Centre Street" purportedly being his first. In any case *The Line-Up* is a wonderful representative of the 1930s police procedural. Interesting, isn't it, that there is now a new police/court procedural TV series set in New York City called *100 Centre Street*? It seems good ideas stay around forever. And, come to think of it, McKee reminds me a bit of Frank Furillo from *Hill Street Blues*.

The Line-Up centers upon the charming Chris McKee, inspector of police in New York City, and his determined attempts to unravel what at first seems to be an only minimally suspicious death. One death leads to another, and thence to an earlier death originally thought to be accidental. The ending is extremely satisfying, and the story is not slow-moving despite the attention to detail.

There is gentle humor here, strong plotting, great descriptive touches. Reilly obviously knew police procedure and conveys her enjoyment of particulars; while her style is descriptive and illuminating it is not dry or boring. Much of the story takes place during the Christmas season during a snowstorm, and she makes you feel as though you are walking in the city, or driving in the country, participating in the chase, surviving the winter weather, experiencing the cold and forceful wind. A likable protagonist, strong plot, great settings — this enjoyable murder mystery has all the right stuff.

Reilly wrote thirty-one Christopher McKee novels, beginning in 1930 and ending in 1962, with her death. Her work improves with age. The last book in the series, *The Day She Died,* is stunning in its suspense. Reilly didn't lose a beat in thirty years.

Kathleen Riley

The Latimer Mercy by Robert Richardson (1985)

I picked up *The Latimer Mercy* years ago because the author's name was the same as my late uncle's. I was also taken with the appealing cover, an illuminated manuscript on the British paperback version. Being a librarian and a lover of rare books, how could I lose? To my delight this is the first of a series (there are now six) starring Augustus Maltravers as the witty protagonist.

None other than Dame P.D. James calls the book "an impressive debut" and Maltravers "a genuine original." Britain's Crime Writers Association must have loved it, too, since they voted it the John Creasey Award for Best First Crime Novel of 1985.

Richardson describes Maltravers thusly:

He was a tall, angular man whose movements fell just short of clumsiness. Beneath erratic brown hair was a long face which seemed to have lived only the summers of his thirty-four years; what had been irritatingly youthful features ten years earlier were becoming increasingly advantageous with the passage of time.

Maltravers is also a playwright of some renown. He comes to Vercaster, a tranquil cathedral town, to direct Diana Porter, a famous actress with an infamous past, in a one-woman show during the newly resurrected Vercaster Arts Festival. Diana, a success on stage and on television, was captured by British tabloids in the nude. So it is with some trepidation that Maltravers presents Diana's show in the exquisite medieval chapter house next to his brother-in-law Michael's cathedral.

Richardson sets the scene:

The three faces of the Chapter House to the south and west flamed as the early evening sun pulled down all the colours of the world. Over the hour and a half of Diana's performance, the light would imperceptibly fade, the audience's eyes adjusting without notice until they were watching the climax in lavender gloom. Maltravers had counted on the additional dramatic effect, with its changing emphasis on glass and stone.

Maltravers, Diana, and Maltravers' lover Tess lodge with his sister Melissa and her husband Michael, the rector, in "God's desirable detached property." The rehearsal goes well, but soon Maltravers is summoned when a valuable and irreplaceable Bible, the Latimer Mercy, is stolen from its case in the cathedral. This is a misprinted version of a 1546 Bible in which the erroneous "merry" in Psalm 25, verse 10, has been hand-corrected to "mercy," reportedly by Bishop Hugh Latimer.

Maltravers is grilled about the robbery by a highly literate detective, and helps Michael in dealing with the press.

In spite of Maltravers' worries, Diana's show portraying women in the bible goes off without a hitch to raves from the audience including the bishop's wife. The dean of the cathedral hosts a blissful tea party in honor of Diana's performance. Amid the crush of partygoers, Diana, like the Latimer Mercy, mysteriously goes missing.

The mood of the book shifts at this point from cozy to thriller as Maltravers and Tess travel from one end of Britain to the other in search of Diana, her supposed abductor and the missing Latimer Mercy.

Beware, this is not for the faint of heart. This is one of my favorite contemporary traditional mysteries. All the elements are there, and like Agatha Christie, the thorns are just beneath the surface — ready to harm the innocent.

Kathy Harig

The Man in Lower Ten by Mary Roberts Rinehart (1909)

A well-heeled lawyer discovers a body in his Pullman berth, breaks his arm in a train wreck, is confronted by a charge of murder, and falls in love.

Hitchcock thriller? Grisham's latest?

Nope. Published nearly a century ago, *The Man in Lower Ten* is the second novel by Mary Roberts Rinehart, one of the most successful American mystery writers of the twentieth century. Most cite her first novel, *The Circular Staircase*, for particular praise, but *The Man in Lower Ten* deserves a look for its twisty plot, delirious amateur sleuthing, and main character's transformation from lonely lawyer to intrepid champion.

Thirty-year-old Washington attorney Lawrence Blakeley is enclosed in a placid existence, ruled by his martinet housekeeper and vaguely unsettled by the feeling, "is that all there is?" A trip to Pittsburgh catapults him into danger, murder, loud clothing not his own, the pursuit of stolen forged documents vital to his current case, and an encounter with a mysterious young woman that the confirmed bachelor finds compelling.

Blakeley is abetted by his mischievous but loyal partner Richey McKnight and the diminutive Wilson Budd Hotchkiss, an amateur detective devoted to scribbling in his notebook and "that inductive method originated by Poe and followed since with such success by Conan Doyle." Along the way there are strange lights in the house next door, blackmail attempts, police scrutiny, and break-ins engineered by the reluctant Blakeley, the obstreperous McKnight, and the enterprising Hotchkiss, armed with a variety of implements from poker to stiletto. But Blakeley is most of all comically and repeatedly put out by the lack of appropriate attire. "Do I look like a man who would wear this kind of a necktie?" he inquires. "Do you suppose I carry purple and green barred silk handkerchiefs?"

More than 20 editions of *The Man in Lower Ten* have been published, but the first edition features vivid and romantic illustrations by Howard Chandler Christy, best known for his World War I bond posters and the mural in the US Capitol, *The Signing of the Constitution.*

Despite a few jarring elements (some sentimental asides and a servant referred to as a "Jap," for example), Rinehart's novel still speaks to readers today in its portrait of a man who remakes himself and risks life and livelihood for the truth and the sake of a damsel in distress. And there are other aspects that the modern reader might find appealing. "You want the unvarnished and ungarnished truth," says McKnight to Blakeley, "and I'm no hand for that. I'm a lawyer."

Elizabeth Foxwell

Chicken Little Was Right by Jean Ruryk (1994)

My favorite underappreciated book is *Chicken Little Was Right* by Jean Ruryk. It was written because her nephew pushed her into a computer class, and at age 67, Ruryk was having problems catching on. As a way of mastering the machine, she decided to use it to write a mystery. The first Cat Wilde book, *Chicken Little Was Right*, was the result. Using her knowledge of buying and selling antiques and managing a Sunday antiques flea market in Montreal, Ruryk created amateur sleuth Cat Wilde, a sixtysomething antique furniture restorer who was a composite of herself and her original partner in the antiques business.

When we meet Cat Wilde, she has just lost her daughter and son-in-law in an automobile accident and is about to lose her house to her son-in-law's parents. Desperate, she decides to rob a bank. Cat's life only gets more complicated when she is approached by a mobster who knows she's the bank robber and threatens to take his proof to the police unless Cat hides a tape recorder in an enemy's house. Cat agrees and later learns it wasn't a tape recorder she hid but something much deadlier.

The plot in *Chicken Little Was Right* is well done and engrossing, but it's her characters I fell in love with. Cat, a warm, nurturing person who cooks for friends and takes in strays, has an engaging, laid-back personality. The funny and lovable Charlie and Rafe, gay antique dealers, are based on two men Ruryk knew in her advertising copywriter days at Young & Rubicam. "They were only supposed to appear in one chapter of the first book," Ruryk said when I interviewed her several years ago, "but they sort of took over and I couldn't let them go." Then there's Mike Melnyk, a curmudgeonly ex-newspaper columnist with a poignant personal history, and Larry Mendelsohn, a very minor character in *Chicken Little* who becomes a pivotal character in *Whatever Happened to Jennifer Steele?* (1996). And Rena, a minor flea market character in the first two books, becomes a major character in the third book, *Next Week Will Be Better* (1998).

Ruryk said she repeated characters from book to book because she wanted her readers to feel they knew Cat's life and knew the people she knew. At the time of her death in 1999, Ruryk was working on the fourth Cat Wilde mystery. Gordon Chase, a minor character in *Next Week Will Be Better*, was to become a major character in the unfinished book. By using a group of ongoing characters and enlarging minor characters into future major characters, Ruryk created a believable, if slightly unusual, world which I think you'll enjoy as much as I have.

Jan Dean

The Hotel Detective by Alan Russell (1994)

Tucking into Am Caulfield's detecting debut is a sublime pleasure. It is like reading the funniest Kinky Friedman but without all the offensive matter. No references to Christians or Jews here, just a whole lot of bedroom humor and wacky situations arising from the commingling of guests and staff at La Jolla's fictional Hotel California.

The story opens with the assistant general manager ruminating on what drew him to the hotel trade in the first place. Am Caulfield has spent the better part of his life serving the needs of others in the comfort industry and one soon learns a lot about Am and his devotion to his job. The astute reader may surmise that a lot of that pride of place, that hunger for novelty, that passion for justice and fair play that spur Am onward are actually reflections of the attitudes held by the author himself. Alan Russell is a 20-plus-year veteran of the California hotel industry.

He's certainly got the credentials to write about innkeeping California style. In addition, he knows how to spin out a yarn that will keep readers riveted to the page. Caulfield's odious boss calls him in to announce his impending vacation, leaving Am in charge of the hotel in his absence. The onerous taskmaster then mentions that the security director quit that same day so Am will also have charge of those duties. In addition, he's hired an intern to assist Am on his rounds, a know-it-all from his alma mater who will tangle with Am from their first meeting.

Am and his intern soon find themselves investigating a suicide, double homicides and the theft of an exotic dancer's frilly, full-figured underwear. And what about that missing laundry and the theft of $3000 worth of designer desserts? Hotel spies, liquor tampering and a convention of 176 people all claiming the name Bob Johnson add exciting complications to the cases.

The New York Times cited Russell for his "gift for dialog" in its review. Aspiring writers and curious readers should also applaud his vocabulary and use of point of view. Making this a third person narrative allows the author a certain omniscience and the freedom to draw information from all quarters. Am's voice is soon joined by the murderer's in the telling and Russell manages to make the murder seem almost accidental and the killer a sympathetic victim of circumstance. Of particular interest, too, are the many ways Russell has his characters refer to the hotel: as a person, as a place, as a destination and an oasis. In each instance his definition is imbued with warmth and possibility.

If there is anything to decry about this work it is that it ended too soon. *The Hotel Detective* and its sequel *The Fat Innkeeper* are the only evidence of Am Caulfield's existence. Would there were more!

Geraldine Galentree

Wilde West by Walter Satterthwait (1991)

Is it a slasher novel? Psychological suspense? A comedy of manners? *Wilde West* includes elements of all of these. What can you say about a crime novel whose jacket proclaims it "a brilliant novel that includes, as all books should, murder, sex, insanity, cannibalism, and a herd of goats"? When it is written by Walter Satterthwait, and it features Oscar Fingal O'Flahertie Wills Wilde, plenty! Satterthwait's third mystery (after the debut of his Joshua Croft series, *At Ease With the Dead*, and his marvelous and thought-provoking *Miss Lizzie*) is an engaging and gently mocking look at Oscar Wilde during his 1882 lecture tour of the American West.

Wilde is in Denver when a red-headed prostitute is found brutally murdered. Down-on-his-luck Federal Marshal Bob Grigsby comes to have information that other ladies who are free with their favors have been butchered in a similar manner in several of the cities where Wilde has lectured, and so believes that either Wilde or one of his party is the killer. Wilde decides to uncover the killer himself — using "a systematic application of the poetic imagination."

Wilde's traveling party includes a number of Christie-esque characters — a hard-drinking newspaperman, an amorous countess, a dreamy young poet, an avaricious businessman, a German colonel and Wilde's negro valet. Satterthwait includes real-life characters in the persons of the infamous John "Doc" Holliday, gambler and gunfighter, who always seems to appear at just the right time and Elizabeth McCourt "Baby" Doe, the voluptuous knockout of a divorcée who is engaged to one of Colorado's richest silver barons and who charms the socks (not to mention the rest of the finery) off Wilde.

Beginning with a prolog that could have been wrenched from the chronicles of Jack the Ripper, most of the action in *Wilde West* occurs at the kind of sites we all know from TV westerns like *Gunsmoke* — saloons, trains, hotel rooms and opera houses. Make no mistake, though, this is not the story of Marshall Dillon and Miss Kitty!

For me, the attraction and joy of this book is the exposition of the character of Oscar Wilde in the hands of a talented storyteller like Satterthwait. The dialog sparkles and the prose reflects a cynical and worldly view of Satterthwait's fictional universe. In the hands of a less skilled writer, the storyline of *Wilde West* could easily have become commonplace and hackneyed. But Satterthwait's writing virtually crackles with vitality. The solution to the murders was less important to me than the unraveling of the characters, who are not all who they appear to be.

The late Barry W. Gardner, fan and reviewer extraordinaire, said of Satterthwait that *Wilde West* "may be his most ambitious novel, and his best." I agree completely, and hope that if you enjoy your history with generous helpings of maniacal crime, fastidious dressing, witty dialog, and lively writing, you will seek out *Wilde West.*

Chris Aldrich

The Concrete River by John Shannon (1996)

In *The Concrete River,* John Shannon begins a series that is a literary examination of the political and social tensions of America's urban future — Southern California. His character, Jack Liffey, represents both the past and the future of the area: a laid-off aerospace worker turned investigator into the disappearance of children. There is a surrealistic quality to the writing and the situations that reminds me of the movie *Blade Runner*, with its post-apocalypse, polyglot society. It is of note that Shannon has received rave reviews in the British press for this series; perhaps it takes a foreign perspective to show us those best at delineating American society.

Shannon takes Jack Liffey into the Southern California neighborhoods that one sees from the freeways, from the San

Fernando Valley to Orange County, each with its distinctive ethnic identity and its own kind of alienation and despair. He is masterful in his ability to create characters who are at once individuals and representatives of different groups. Whether he is presenting a Mexican mother, a Hollywood starlet, an out-of-work aerospace worker, or a Vietnamese refugee, Shannon gives us a picture of a real person, caught up in a situation where the California Dream has turned to a nightmare.

It is the Los Angeles River, covered in concrete and garbage, that is the symbol of this soulless and unnatural place of strip malls and tract houses. Jack Liffey is a contemporary Philip Marlowe, true to an old-fashioned code of justice and fair play. In *Concrete River,* Shannon gives us a world where the only value is to treat each other as human beings in the face of the relentless dehumanization of the environment. Jack is hired by a Mexican woman whose daughter is missing, only to find out that the daughter has been drowned. Jack joins forces with an activist former nun when it becomes clear that the death was murder and is related to the work that the daughter was doing in the neighborhood.

In all of Shannon's novels, the plots center around greed. Even the destructive power of nature is unleashed by human greed. The villains who murder and steal from the poor and the defenseless are the psychotic henchmen for those most psychotic and soulless of contemporary villains: big corporations. There is an apocalyptic quality to Shannon's vision: for example, in *The Poison Sky*, the entire San Fernando Valley is devastated by a toxic gas leak. This is the raw strength of Shannon's writing: he can create relentless evil. When the serial killer is a real estate developer or a toxic-waste-spewing chemical company, in comparison even Hannibal Lecter comes across as a pussycat. This examination of the nature of evil, along with an ability to write first-rate prose, is what places Shannon's work in the top rank of *fin de siecle* American mystery.

Christine Acevedo

Never Quite Dead by Seymour Shubin (1989)

Wasn't the son of spies the CIA knew about but couldn't reveal, or a guinea pig in a scientist's experiments, or the president's hidden illegitimate child.
He was... just a kid.

In this beautifully written novel of mystery and suspense, the search for truth and the search for self move on parallel paths. A little boy's body is found in a vacant lot. He was a beautiful little boy, well dressed and cared for. Who killed him and why, in more than twenty years after he was found murdered, had no one ever come forward to say his name? Surely someone knew where he lived, where he played, who he was.

The story begins in Boston, where Joseph Kyle, a newspaper columnist, cannot let the story die. As the years pass, the police see him as an obsessed old man, pursuing a long dead case, long grown cold, when a final clue takes him to Philadelphia. Before he can complete his investigation, he dies and his son, David, is driven to continue the search. David Kyle is a respected author of thrillers who never expected to be involved in any true crime situation. But he follows in his father's footsteps, thus resolving the rivalry between a living child and a dead one and the relationship between a father and son. The climax of the action takes place at the Jersey shore. It may be unexpected but all the clues are there in this well-crafted psychological maze.

Seymour Shubin writes about situations or events that he feels strongly about and that have meaning for him. *Never Quite Dead* is based on an actual event in Philadelphia — a murder that affected a whole community, from the coroner's assistant who spent much of his life attempting to identify "the boy in the box," to the policemen who paid for a little headstone in Potter's Field, to each parent who held his child a little closer. In a sense, this book is a gift to "the boy in the box," and a true gem of compelling psychological suspense.

157

Shubin is one of Philadelphia's senior authors and one of America's most gifted writers of psychological suspense. A journalism graduate of Temple University, he has written twelve novels and hundreds of articles and short fiction for such magazines as the Saturday Evening Post, Reader's Digest, Redbook and Ellery Queen's Mystery Magazine. His first novel, *Anyone's My Name*, was published in 1953 and made the New York Times bestseller list. Recent novels include *The Good and the Dead, Fury's Children* and *My Face Among Strangers*.

Deen Kogan

Nine Coaches Waiting by Mary Stewart (1959)

The 1960s and 1970s were the heyday of the romantic suspense novel, often scornfully called "the Gothic." Because many of these books featured young woman in frightening situations and involved romance with a man who might or might not be the villain, critics often derided them. There were many really bad books published in this genre, but Mary Stewart was one of the writers (along with Phyllis A. Whitney, Victoria Holt and Barbara Michaels/Elizabeth Peters) who wrote romantic suspense that showed just how good these books could be.

Stewart began her career in 1955 with *Madam, Will You Talk?*, set in Provence. There is a sense of immediacy about Stewart's descriptions of place, and I never have any difficulty picturing the setting as I read. The gloomy and isolated chateau of Valmy, the heart *of Nine Coaches Waiting*, is a case in point. As in all her books, Stewart cleverly uses the setting to heighten the suspense.

The Stewart "heroine" is generally a young Englishwoman of good, solid middle-class stock. Often she is well-educated, but she doesn't have many financial resources, so she has to find a job. Sometimes this involves looking after children, as in Stewart's fourth novel, *Nine Coaches Waiting*. Linda Martin, the heroine, is intelligent and sensitive. Though young, she has a good insight into character and behavior, which serves her well. She is mature in many ways, though she is somewhat lacking in self-confidence in certain areas.

Linda acts as governess and companion to young Philippe, the Comte de Valmy. Though this is a stereotypical role for a woman, Linda turns out to have the inner resources of courage and strength of purpose needed to save herself and Philippe. At the end of the novel, she does ride off into the sunrise with the dark and brooding "hero," but Stewart uses the element of romance to heighten the suspense. Will Raoul de Valmy turn out to be a bad guy, and will Linda end up in the arms of the sturdy Englishman, William Blake? Or will Raoul turn out to be a good guy after all?

Stewart and her peers wrote about women coping with their lives in the circumstances the best way they could. The writers and their heroines were very much products of their culture, which was a good bit more conservative than our society today. To me, these women were the equivalent of the male adventurers like James Bond. Women writers chose to set their stories on a more personal and intimate stage, while the men usually went for something epic and global. As far as I'm concerned, the James Bond novels are as much "romantic suspense" as anything Stewart wrote. Men, in order to fulfill their destiny as saviors of the world, have to have adventures on an epic scale, like those impenetrable technothrillers Tom Clancy writes. Women are more interested in saving a small part of the world at a time, even if it means simply saving the life of a child so he can grow up to enjoy his inheritance from his parents, as in *Nine Coaches Waiting*.

Dean James

The Left Leg by Alice Tilton (1940)

Alice Tilton is one of the two pseudonyms used by Phoebe Atwood Taylor. (She also wrote one book as Freeman Dana: *Murder at the New York World's Fair*.) Her books written under her true name of Phoebe Atwood Taylor feature Asey Mayo, the Cape Cod Sherlock. I am a fan of humorous books, so I chose to write here about the antics of Leonidas Witherall. Leonidas is nicknamed Bill due to his striking resemblance to William Shakespeare. He has had many jobs, including teaching school. He also secretly writes the popular Haseltine series of books and radio adventures.

This series may well be described as caper novels. The humor quotient is set very high. The situations Bill gets into would try the patience of a saint, while readers just try to keep from laughing out loud, especially if reading the books in public. While I reread *The Left Leg* to write this article, the joys of reading Tilton came rushing back. I will need to read the entire series again.

The Left Leg is set in WWII New England. Bill is on his way home from visiting a former teaching colleague. His bus ride is cut short when a young woman accuses him of annoying her. Bill dubs her the Scarlet Wimpernel due to her red attire. She is intent on following him, an action that makes no sense given her accusations.

Bill is trying to get to a friend's house after being ejected from the bus when he is accused of robbing a hardware store. The theft was actually done by a man dressed in a leprechaun suit carrying a gilded harp.

Bill gets to his friend's home in a crazy fashion and stumbles over his body. He discovers his friend had an artificial left leg, which has gone missing.

While the stories take place in the kinder, gentler 1930s and 1940s, they are not really dated. There is a somewhat cozy, homey feel to the series. There are some references to dungarees, and in one scene, Bill helps the Wimpernel put her bus ticket stub in the slot of the seat in front of her. This type of detail, and the lack of sex and violence, show the difference in periods of our country's history.

Humorous books don't always get the respect or attention they deserve, but they are a sure fire way to pass a pleasant afternoon sitting in a comfy chair, sipping a favorite beverage and scaring the pet on your lap by frequent chortles of laughter. Tilton will make you laugh with the best of them, and is most worthy of discovery. While I prefer to read books in order, each book stands on its own. As they may be out of print, grab any you can find. I highly recommend all in the series.

Maggie Mason

Just What the Doctor Ordered by Colin Watson (1969) aka The Flaxborough Crab

Reading *Just What the Doctor Ordered* is like being seated front and center at a comic drama. In act one, women are accosted by elderly gentlemen who scuttle off sideways, like crabs. A woman in a church hears a man telling her that she has "a lovely white bottom." Detective Inspector Purbright's attempts to trap the miscreants end with the comedy of the trapper trapped. When Alderman Winge chases — "coming sideways on" — Bertha Pollock, then falls in a reservoir and drowns, Purbright assumes the case is over.

In act two, further unusual sexual behavior by old, sidling men forces Purbright and Detective Sergeant Love to reopen the investigation. Inquiries lead to a doctor and to an herb farm that makes Samson's Salad, reputed to "impart the sexual virility of the Ancient Britons." The director, Miss Lucilla Edith Cavill Teatime, fearing sales will be affected, begins her own investigation into the case of the staggering, randy men. The act ends with murder.

In act three, we see parallel investigations by Purbright and the ever resourceful Miss Teatime. They arrive at the same conclusion, with Purbright deciphering a verbal clue (as clever as any of Christie's) and Teatime recognizing the physical evidence against the murderer.

Each act consists of six chapters. Evidence suggests that Watson is a careful craftsman, attentive to broad structure and to the most minor detail. Such detail is evident in his creation of village life. As in classic drama, the bucolic surface is suggested by names: Butters, Sweeting, Meadow, Cowper, Bellweather. But Watson also has great fun at boldly hinting at the underlying erotic life. He plays with place names: Hoare's Sluice; with old plant names: poke-me-gently, tickle-titty, purple lechery, maids-in-a-sweat, and even with the naming of Chief Constable Chubb's dog, Six-Shot Rufus.

In most comedies underneath physical activities lie serious concerns. The subjects here are doctors, money and social pretensions. Watson satirizes such people as the doctor's wife, with her three-tone doorbell and a hat which is "a sure sign of social status." Under the glittering surface of recent affluence and class elevation is grim greed, as true for the doctor's wife as it is for the herbmaster Holy Joe. The inhabitants of this world try to cover up greed and envy just as businessmen cover up unethical practices. This is grist for a satirist's mill. It is also a world in which Miss Teatime survives, moving like a water bug skittering over the surface, because she can see what is below.

Watson's broad comedy may at first seem a mild broth, but it ends as a rather spicy stew. The novel is a fount of pre-Viagra geriatric wit. And it's a pleasure to savor once again this writer with a Chandleresque sense of simile: Constable Braine has "all the dash of a monumental mason with arthritis." Tea is "like concentrated wood preservative," and Miss Pollock's hat the "color of lips in heart failure."

Gordon Magnuson

Sleep Long, My Love by Hillary Waugh (1959)

A dismembered and crudely disemboweled female body concealed in a trunk is almost a commonplace in mystery fiction, but the desperation and brutality implied by such a murder comes as a real surprise to the cops of Stockford, Connecticut. *Sleep Long, My Love*, a representative entry in the fine series featuring police chief Fred Fellows, gets its considerable energy and excitement from the contrast between the horrific and baffling homicide and the rational, methodical work of law enforcement. Like his contemporary Joseph Harrington, Hilary Waugh uses the police novel to illustrate, even celebrate, how order and procedure can thwart, or at least bring to judgment, those who yield to violent desires.

Waugh sets his series firmly in a suburbia that anyone who was alive in the '60s will instantly recognize. His fictional Stockford suggests Bethel or Brookfield, Connecticut; it's a town increasingly populated by New York City commuters, just losing its small-town feeling, with neighbors slightly less likely to know the folks next door. In each novel, after the discovery of the crime, the narrative focus turns to the tedious business of investigation; Waugh reminds us how much police work takes place on the phone, with policemen crossing off names in the directory one by one, eliminating possible victims or employers or witnesses. The clues always appear to be provocative dead ends — a new trunk marked only with initials, a photograph of a nameless woman — and Fellows's deductions are always plausible but clever. (One exception occurs in *Sleep Long, My Love*; Fellows makes a completely unreasonable assumption about a name on a pad of paper, but that's an anomaly.)

In addition to detailing the quest for the killer, the novels also briefly explore the emotional response of the male cops to the crimes and to the victims, who are usually attractive women; and they register the policemen's difficult relationship with the press. The novels tend to end with a bang, as the criminal is trapped or exposed with dramatic flourish. The denouement of *Sleep Long, My Love* is particularly neat and unexpected. In addition to *Sleep Long, My Love*, good entries in this series include *The Missing Man, Pure Poison* and *The Late Mrs. D.*

Another early Waugh novel that deserves special mention is *Last Seen Wearing*, originally published in Cosmopolitan in 1952. Set in Massachusetts and featuring a cynical police chief called Frank Ford, it reads like a dry run for the Fellows series. The novel begins with the disappearance of a pretty student from a prestigious women's college: was it abduction? elopement? murder? suicide? Again, the novel derives its power from the conjunction of the procedural machinery and the deductive brilliance of the central investigator, with, as is often true of the Fellows novels as well, just enough of a sexual frisson (late '50s style) to keep the pages turning. If you're looking for a fairly plotted and exciting American procedural, few writers were more readable and reliable than Hilary Waugh in the 1960s.

Lisa Berglund

Kahawa by Donald E. Westlake (1982)

Scouting out the abandoned railway spur where they will (temporarily) hide the coffee train they plan to steal from Idi Amin, Isaac (ex-Ugandan civil servant, family slaughtered by Amin for ... well, no reason, really) and Frank (ex-pat mercenary) park the Mercedes in which they infiltrated Uganda (in disguise) on the old access road, now overgrown by the jungle. Isaac is struck by the fact that it looks as if they're in a photo-shoot for a luxury car ad. "Now I know why they were there, their drivers were stealing coffee." And after reading this marvelous book, you will want to go steal kahawa (coffee in Swahili) too.

Donald Westlake puts the ball in play with a gloriously

intricate plot. Idi Amin has to sell the coffee to get the hard currency he needs to provide the thugs that keep him in power with the luxuries that keep them happy. One of Amin's henchman (Chase) plots the heist so as to leave Uganda in style, as things are getting so crazy that Amin might actually turn on *him*. Chase contacts an Indian merchant in neighboring Kenya who can both put together a team to steal the train and launder (as it were) the coffee, while, of course, plotting to double cross him with the assistance of the principal of the Swiss/German hedge fund that's financing Amin's sale, who is ... you get the idea. But, of course, as Helmut Von Moltke almost put it: no plot survives contact with the enemy. The story then emerges from the scheming and improvising the plotters must do when all of these myriad plots collide.

While the story alone makes *Kahawa* a brilliant thriller, the characters and the writing elevate *Kahawa* into a brilliant novel, full stop. Indeed, one imagines that Westlake put *Kahawa* together only by winning a fierce bidding war with V.S. Naipaul for even the most minor characters.

In one scene Lew (another of the mercenaries) must fetch a shipment of sewing machines that have gone astray. (Arriving at the depot, he finds that the terminal manager and the freightmaster have been so busy stealing them from one another (so as to collect the bribe needed to release them) that they allowed a third party to steal the machines from both of them. Since losing goods altogether is definitely bad form, the freightmaster offers to "accidentally deliver" (for a small consideration) a consignment of outboard motors to the merchant instead (the true owner of which has been jailed and so won't be looking for them). One small scene, yet it perfectly captures just why it is that economists now believe that corruption is the single biggest factor preventing economic development in the third world.

And here is one of the characters describing Port Victoria (a port on the lake between Kenya and Uganda): "In addition to the ghostly echo of what might have been, there was also the hidden face of corruption…in losing its original destiny, Port Victoria had become … almost like a failed person… 'It's a Graham Greene character as geography.'"

So, just as people share 98% of their DNA with chimpanzees, *Kahawa* shares many of its base constituents with other thrillers. And the difference is as marked. One should read *Kahawa* just to see what thrillers can be.

Kevin James

A Cool Breeze on the Underground by Don Winslow (1991)

This strong series kickoff (Edgar nominee for Best First Novel) introduces us to Neal Carey in 1976. We catch up with him in grad school, but Don Winslow supplies a rich background on how the bastard son of a strung-out hooker comes to be attending Columbia, studying English literature, and handling sensitive assignments for Ethan Kitteredge, head of a powerful New England banking family.

Neal's mentor is Joe "Dad" Graham, a PI long on savvy but short on class. Until recently, he supervised Friends of the Family, a little known department of The Bank. This clandestine service was created to discreetly put out fires for its esteemed clients. Now Ed Levine, originally an ambitious underling, is running the show. But Graham is teaching Neal everything he knows. And Kitteredge is grooming Neal to mingle in polite society and ultimately take over Friends, dealing with troubled blue bloods at their own level.

Senator John Chase faces a major PR problem. The Democratic convention is coming up and Chase is hoping to be tapped as the vice-presidential nominee. He wants to present a solid family values front on the podium. Unfortunately, his 17-year-old daughter Allie has a colorful past replete with drug and alcohol abuse, boarding school expulsions and sexual promiscuity. Now she's disappeared, last sighted in London by a school friend. Neal's mission is to find the girl, clean her up, and deliver her to her parents before August 1. Keep the authorities completely out of it. Levine is skeptical, Neal reluctant, and Dad hopes for the best.

London is a big city and Neal needs all his skills to find the runaway girl. That's only the beginning, though. Allie's fallen in with a bad crowd and her new friends are trouble. Then complications arise from a very unexpected source.

The mystery — a cat and mouse story within a cat and mouse story — is a solid start for this excellent series. The education of Neal Carey, a young street kid, is equally compelling. PI Joe "Dad" Graham takes the neophyte pickpocket under his wing and turns the gifted amateur into a talented professional. Neal learns how to tail someone without being made, how to climb stairs and get through windows silently, the best way to search a room, and other essential survival techniques. Dad knows whereof he speaks. Nothing is wasted. The relationship between Graham and the boy is truly patriarchal. In everything but DNA, Dad is a strict but loving parent.

The characters are well drawn and the dialog suitable for the smart mouth of an independent 23-year-old and uptight authority figures unaccustomed to being questioned. But it's Winslow's way with words that provides a truly worthy showcase. "Like aging women, cities are prettier at night. The softer light shades the insults of aging. Darkness fades the lines and wrinkles that every good woman and every good city wear on their faces as signs that somebody has lived there." That's a London the reader can embrace. Whether it's mean little one-armed leprechauns or undercover operatives distracted by a rare book, you'll be lured through the entire five book series and scanning the new releases for another adventure.

Beth Fedyn

Contributors

Christine Acevedo, who read her first Nancy Drew at age six, was a stockbroker for 17 years before becoming a co-owner of Clues Unlimited. She is the owner of Sophie the mystery pig, Clues Unlimited's mascot. Essays: *Rough Cut* by Stan Cutler & *The Concrete River* by John Shannon.

> **Clues Unlimited**, 123 South Eastbourne Ave, Tucson, AZ 85716. Phone: 520-326-8533. Email: info@cluesunlimited.com. Website: www.cluesunlimited.com.

Robin & Jamie Agnew own & operate Aunt Agatha's mystery bookstore in Ann Arbor, Michigan. Formerly residents of Minneapolis, Minnesota, Uncle Edgar's mystery bookstore there presented such an agreeable life plan, complete with playpen and baby in the store, that it seemed wise to follow. Now we have our own two babies (grown out of the playpen), are reading as many mysteries as we can get our hands on, and are raising our children to do the same. Essays: *Good Cop, Bad Cop* by Barbara D'Amato (Robin), *Jitterbug* by Loren D. Estleman (Robin) & *The Dogs of Winter* by Kem Nunn (Jamie).

> **Aunt Agatha's**, 213 South 4th Avenue, Ann Arbor, MI 48104. Phone: 734-769-1114. Email: WENGAS@aol.com. Website: www.auntagathas.com.

Chris Aldrich became addicted to mysteries at an early age and took her first steps towards outright fanaticism in 1995 when she discovered the CompuServe mystery forum. There she met others who share her madness, including her evil twin and Mystery News partner, Lynn Kaczmarek. Essay: *Wilde West* by Walter Satterthwait.

> **Mystery News**, Black Raven Press, PMB 152, 105 Town Line

Rd, Vernon Hills, IL 60061. Phone: 917-405-3613. Email: caldrich@blackravenpress.com. Web: www.blackravenpress.com.

Josephine A. Bayne became addicted to mysteries at age eight when her mother read her *The Murder of Roger Ackroyd*, while living in Florence, Italy. Bayne was a finalist in a recent St. Martin's/Malice Domestic Contest, and is at work on another Venetian mystery. Her essays are dedicated to the memory of Eva Cooper, mystery lover and friend. Essays: *The Stately Home Murder* by Catherine Aird & *Envious Casca* by Georgette Heyer.

Mystery Books, 916 W. Lancaster Ave, Bryn Mawr, PA 19010. Phone: 610-526-9993. Email: mysterybooks@earthlink.net. Website: www.mysterybooksonline.com.

Lisa Berglund is a professor in the English department at SUNY-Buffalo State College. Her published research includes articles on Johnson, Boswell, Tennyson and 17th century drama, and she is editing Hester Lynch Piozzi's (Mrs. Thrale's) Anecdotes of Samuel Johnson. She has been a member of the Drood Review staff since 1984. Essays: *The Last Known Address* by Joseph Harrington & *Sleep Long, My Love* by Hillary Waugh.

Kate Birkel is the founder/owner of the Mystery Bookstore in Omaha, NE. A reader from her earliest years, she reads mysteries, science fiction, history and the backs of cereal boxes in emergencies. Her other hobby is counted thread needlework, and she would really appreciate at least one extra day in the week. Essay: *Bridge of Birds* by Barry Hughart.

The Mystery Bookstore, 1422 S. 13th St., Omaha, NE 68108. Phone: 888-412-7343. Email: hudunit@radiks.net. Website: www.mysterybookstore.ws.

Bonnie Claeson has been selling mystery books for 16 years and has co-owned The Black Orchid Bookshop with her partner Joseph Guglielmelli for seven of them. Essay: *Falling Angel* by William Hjortsberg.

> **The Black Orchid Bookshop**, 303 E. 81st St, New York, NY 10028. Phone: 212-734-5980. Email: Borchid@aol.com. Website: www.ageneralstore.com.

From Grand Rapids, Michigan, **Jo Ellyn Clarey** mixes the fun of history-mystery with her academic work on issues in narrative. Currently, she is editing collections of author interviews and essays studying the gender/genre upheavals occasioned by female sleuths in historical settings. Essay: *Irene's Last Waltz* by Carole Nelson Douglas.

Melanie Meyers Cushman lives in New York City, and works at Murder Ink, the world's oldest mystery bookstore, with her husband, Tom Cushman. She thinks that she, Tom, son Jack, and their pets would fit right into Blue Deer with no problems at all. Essay: *The Edge of the Crazies* by Jamie Harrison.

> **Murder Ink**, 2486 Broadway, New York, NY 10025. Phone: 212-362-8123. Email: info@MurderInk.com. Website: www.MurderInk.com.

Patricia Davis started by reading her parents' Erle Stanley Gardners and Agatha Christies in the first grade. She went on to earn a Ph.D. in English and to teach composition and literature in Tucson's community college for 30 years. She recently retired from teaching to devote full time to the bookstore. Essays: *Done Wrong* by Eleanor Taylor Bland & *Blanche Cleans Up* by Barbara Neely.

> **Clues Unlimited**, 123 South Eastbourne Ave, Tucson, AZ 85716. Phone: 520-326-8533. Email: info@cluesunlimited.com. Website: www.cluesunlimited.com.

Jan Dean, a long-time lover of cozies, especially humorous ones like Jean Ruryk's, publishes the subscription newsletter, Murder Most Cozy, and leads the Cozy Crimes, Cream Teas & Books, Books, Books tours to England every May. Essay: *Chicken Little Was Right* by Jean Ruryk.

Murder Most Cozy, PO Box 561153, Orlando, FL 32856-1153. Phone: 407-481-9481. Email: jandean@bellsouth.net.

Kate Derie is the creator of Cluelass.com, the most popular online reference site for fans of mystery fiction. She is also editor & publisher of *The Deadly Directory 2002*, a guidebook to mystery booksellers, groups, events, periodicals and more. Essays: *Warrant for X* by Philip MacDonald & *Dead Letters* by Sean McGrady.

Deadly Serious Press, 6702 N Casas Adobes Dr, Tucson, AZ 85704-6124. Email: info@deadlyserious.com. Website: www.deadlyserious.com.

Susan Ekholm's love of mystery was probably pre-ordained when she was born on Halloween. A mystery reader since she discovered *The Hound of the Baskervilles* in fifth grade, she was inspired to open A Compleat Mystery Bookshop in coastal Portsmouth, New Hampshire, after reading Carolyn Hart's series about a mystery bookstore. The bookshop closed in early 2002 after almost seven years in business although the website continues at: www.compleatmystery.com. Essay: *Borderlines* by Archer Mayor.

Sue Feder, born talking, learned to read shortly thereafter. She eventually combined these talents by sidling over to people and recommending books. She then pounced upon unsuspecting historical mystery writers by founding The Historical Mystery Appreciation Society. Essays: *Hardly a Man Is Now Alive* by Herbert Brean & *Beyond the Grave* by Marcia Muller & Bill Pronzini.

Historical Mystery Appreciation Society, 3 Goucher Woods Ct, Towson, MD 21286. Email: Monkshould@comcast.net. Website: members.home.net/monkshould.

By day, **Beth Fedyn** works for a bonding agency (no, they don't do bail bonds). Nights and weekends, she sells mysteries at Books & Company, an independent general bookstore in Oconomowoc, Wisconsin. She also reviews for Deadly Pleasures and Mystery News. Essays: *The Butcher's Boy* by Thomas Perry & *A Cool Breeze on the Underground* by Don Winslow.

Books & Company, Whitman Park Shopping Center, 1039 Summit Ave, Oconomowoc, WI 53066. Phone: 262-567-0106. Website: www.booksco.com.

Sally Fellows is a retired high school history teacher with a passion for mysteries. She reviews for Mystery News and for the Mystery Book Store at www.mysterybookstore.ws. Essay: *Working Murder* by Eleanor Boylan.

Ted Fitzgerald reviews and, too infrequently, writes crime fiction. His work has appeared in The Drood Review, Mystery Scene, Hardboiled, and in the anthologies *Private Eyes* (Signet) and *Feline and Famous: Cat Crimes Goes Hollywood* (Donald Fine). Essay: *Laura* by Vera Caspary.

A contributing editor to Mystery Scene, **Elizabeth Foxwell** has published five mystery short stories and edited or co-edited nine anthologies, including *More Murder They Wrote* (Berkley) and *Malice Domestic 10* (Avon). Her website can be found at www.elizabethfoxwell.com. Essays: *Unpunished* by Charlotte Perkins Gilman & *The Man in Lower Ten* by Mary Roberts Rinehart.

Longtime reviewer and bookseller **Geraldine Galentree** is the former manager of The Mystery Book Store in Dallas, Texas (since closed). Geraldine is now the editor of Cozies, Capers & Crimes, A Newsletter for Booklovers available by email and online. Essays: *The Victim in Victoria Station* by Jeanne M. Dams & *The Hotel Detective* by Alan Russell.

Cozies, Capers & Crimes. Email: galentre@mail.airmail.net. Website: http://home.att.net/~csilberblatt/ccc.htm.

Jan Grape won an Anthony and a Macavity, and was nominated for Edgar, Shamus and Agatha awards. Mysteries & More, the Austin bookshop that Jan and her husband Elmer opened in 1990, has ceased operations except for selling Jan's first full-length novel, *Austin City Blue*, published in October 2001 by Five Star Mysteries. Essays: *The Man in the Green Chevy* by Susan Rogers Cooper & *Shackles* by Bill Pronzini.

Jan Grape. Email: Jangrape@aol.com. Website: www.jangrape.com.

Joe Guglielmelli has read mysteries since his fourth grade teacher introduced him to Agatha Christie. He has co-owned The Black Orchid Bookshop with his partner Bonnie Claeson since 1994. Essays: *The Nightrunners* by Joe R. Lansdale & *The Wailing Frail* by Richard S. Prather.

The Black Orchid Bookshop, 303 E. 81st St, New York, NY 10028. Phone: 212-734-5980. Email: Borchid@aol.com. Website: www.ageneralstore.com.

Kathy Harig writes: "I received my Masters in Library Science from Catholic University of America in 1971. I was an Army librarian in Germany from 1971-1974. I have published a book on those experiences, *Libraries, The Military, and Civilian Life*. I was a branch manager with the Enoch Pratt Free Library from 1977 until my retirement in December 2001. I am the co-owner of Mystery Loves Company Booksellers in Baltimore, MD, that I co-founded in 1991." Essays: *Fast Company* by

Marco Page & *The Latimer Mercy* by Robert Richardson.

> **Mystery Loves Company**, 1730 Fleet St, Baltimore, MD
> 21231-2919. Phone: 800-538-0042. Email:
> kathy@mysterylovescompany.com. Website:
> www.mysterylovescompany.com.

Maryelizabeth Hart is an owner and the Publicity Manager for Mysterious Galaxy in San Diego. **Elizabeth Baldwin** is the Inventory Manager. They are actively involved in the Independent Mystery Booksellers Association, with Hart serving as the Director from 2001 to 2003. Their enthusiasm for great fiction is boundless. Essay: *Midnight Baby* by Wendy Hornsby.

> **Mysterious Galaxy**, 7051 Clairemont Mesa Blvd, Suite #302,
> San Diego, CA 92111. Phone: 858-268-4747. Email:
> publicity@mystgalaxy.com. Website: www.mystgalaxy.com.

As a fourth grader, **Jeff Hatfield** would buy Spillane and Fleming by mail and hide them in the attic of his sister's dollhouse. For twenty-one years he's been essentially Uncle Edgar at Uncle Edgar's Mystery and Uncle Hugo's Science Fiction Bookstores in Minneapolis, Minnesota. Essays: *Killing Suki Flood* by Robert Leininger & *A Back Room in Somers Town* by John Malcolm.

> **Uncle Edgar's Mystery Bookstore**, 2864 Chicago Ave S,
> Minneapolis, MN 55407-1320. Phone: 612-824-9984. Email:
> unclehugo@aol.com.

Sandie Herron is a reviewer for www.ILoveAMystery-Newsletter.com and other publications. As the former owner of the independent bookstore A Novel Idea, she especially loves the hypermodern mystery and treasures her personal collection of signed first editions. Essays: *Iron Lake* by William Kent Krueger & *Bird Dog* by Philip Reed.

Sandie Herron, c/o TaxBill Herron, 5590 Bee Ridge Road #3, Sarasota, FL 34233-1505. Email: SandieHerron@att.net.

Jill Hinckley, co-owner of Murder by the Book in Portland, Oregon, decided to start the store, nearly twenty years ago, to feed her own mystery habit. Having her own store also makes a great excuse for never reading anything but mysteries — a tough job, but someone's gotta do it, right? Essays: *A Show of Hands* by David A. Crossman & *Park Lane South, Queens* by Mary Anne Kelly.

Murder by the Book, 3210 SE Hawthorne, Portland, OR 97214. Phone: 503-232-9995. Email: books@mbtb.com. Website: www.mbtb.com.

Jim Huang is the editor of this book, and of The Drood Review. (See page 192.) Essay: *Kill Me Again* by Terence Faherty.

Ken Hughes operates Strange Birds Books out of his home, with the help of his wife Melanie Grace and his computer. He has about 50,000 books in his home, adding more daily, but isn't worried about running out of room, yet. Essay: *Boy's Life* by Robert R. McCammon.

Strange Birds Books, PO Box 12639, Norwood, OH 45212. Phone: 888-917-3336. Email: Strngbirds@aol.com. Website: www.ABEbooks.com/home/strangebirds.

Jeanne M. Jacobson is a frequent contributor to The Drood Review, and rejoices in the possession of an extensive collection of mysteries. The Drs. Jacobson, *mère et fille,* are authors of soon-to-be-published *Detecta-Crostics: Puzzles of Mystery.* Essays: *Without Lawful Authority* by Manning Coles & *Death of the Duchess* by Elizabeth Eyre.

Jennie G. Jacobson is the *fille* mentioned above, although she and husband Jim Huang have two *filles* of their own. Jennie is a medical writer and a managing editor of The Drood Review. Essay: *The Tightrope Walker* by Dorothy Gilman.

Maxim Jakubowski is the owner of London's Murder One, the world's largest mystery bookstore. He is also a crime writer in his own right and known as "the King of the erotic thriller" (dixit The Times), and a prolific anthologist. He is a past winner of the Anthony Award, reviews crime for the Guardian newspaper and is Literary Director of the Crime Scene Film and Literature Festival. Essays: *The Mystery of the Yellow Room* by Gaston Leroux & *I Was Dora Suarez* by Derek Raymond.

> **Murder One**, 71-73 Charing Cross Rd, London, WC2H 0AA ENGLAND. Phone: 44 207 734 3483. Email: murderone.mail@virgin.net. Website: www.murderone.co.uk.

A fan of mysteries since he discovered Nancy Drew at the age of ten, **Dean James** is the co-author of numerous works of mystery non-fiction. He is now writing mysteries of his own, while he continues to manage Murder by the Book in Houston. Essays: *Murders in Volume 2* by Elizabeth Daly & *Nine Coaches Waiting* by Mary Stewart.

> **Murder by the Book**, 2342 Bissonnet, Houston, TX 77005-1512. Phone: 713-524-8597. Email: murderbk@swbell.net. Website: www.murderbooks.com.

Kevin James is a financial economist who spends a considerable proportion of his time solving — so far — blissfully non-violent antitrust and market manipulation cases on behalf of government agencies in the US and the UK. Essay: *Kahawa* by Donald E. Westlake.

Kathryn Kennison is the director of the E.B. and Bertha C. Ball Center at Ball State University, Muncie, Indiana. In 1994, she co-founded Magna Cum Murder: The Mid-America Crime

Fiction Conference. She continues as conference director, and as executive editor of the Magna quarterly Pomp and Circumstantial Evidence. *Essays: Matricide at St. Martha's* by Ruth Dudley Edwards & *The Pew Group* by Anthony Oliver.

Magna Cum Murder, EB & Bertha C Ball Center, Muncie, IN 47306. Phone: 765-285-8975. Email: kennisonk@aol.com. Website: www.magnacummurder.com.

Deen Kogan is active in the mystery field as a producer, reviewer and collector. She chaired the 1989 Bouchercon, with her late husband, Jay; chaired the 1998 event and will chair Bouchercon 2003 in Las Vegas. She also produces the annual Mid-Atlantic Mystery Conference. Essay: *Never Quite Dead* by Seymour Shubin.

Deen Kogan, Detecto Mysterioso, c/o SHP, 507 S 8th St, Philadelphia, PA 19147. Phone: 215-923-0211. Email: shp@erols.com.

Anne Poe Lehr writes: "I come by my love of mystery and detective fiction naturally, since I am a cousin of Edgar Allan Poe and his wife, Virginia Clemm. Visiting with my family in Baltimore I was surrounded by Poe's spirit and writings. The result is Poe's Cousin." Essay: *Not a Creature Was Stirring* by Jane Haddam.

Poe's Cousin, 9 Windward Ave, White Plains, NY 10605-5306. Phone: 914-948-0735. Email: orders@poescousin.com. Website: www.poescousin.com.

Andy Levine considers himself the backbone of Kate's Mystery Books (He hauls boxes, digs holes for tombstones, poses for silhouettes, shovels snow and contributes to the Kate's Mystery Books Newsletter.) In his spare time, he practices law, runs the triathalon and swears he can write a better mystery than most of the ones he has read. He also contributed to *100 Favorite*

Mysteries of the Century. Essay: *Panicking Ralph* by Bill James.

Kate's Mystery Books, 2211 Mass Ave, Cambridge, MA 02140-1211. Phone: 617-491-2660. Email: katesmysbks@earthlink.net. Website: www.katesmysterybooks.com.

Gordon Magnuson has been a collector of mysteries for many years, with emphasis on novels written before 1950. A professor emeritus of English at Virginia Wesleyan College in Norfolk, Virginia, he occasionally writes on topics related to mysteries. He is also the proprietor of Magna Mysteries. Essays: *With a Bare Bodkin* by Cyril Hare & *Just What the Doctor Ordered* by Colin Watson.

Magna Mysteries, PO Box 5732, Virginia Beach, VA 23471. Email: magnamys@pilot.infi.net.

Maggie Mason has been a mystery reader since her childhood, starting with Nancy Drew. Maggie has been a bookseller since 1989, Maggie was the first Fan Guest of Honor at Left Coast Crime in Boulder, Co. and Fan Guest of Honor at Bouchercon in 1999. Maggie reviews mysteries for Deadly Pleasures Magazine. Look for Maggie at most mystery conventions. Essays: *Running Blind* by Lee Child & *The Left Leg* by Alice Tilton.

Lookin for Books, Box 15804, San Diego, CA 92175-5804. Phone: 619-287-2299. Email: maggiemary@yahoo.com.

Kate Mattes has been reading mysteries all her life and selling them at Kate's Mystery Books in Cambridge, Massachusetts, since 1983. She is both editor and reviewer for Kate's Mystery Books Newsletter. Articles and reviews have appeared in *1001 Midnights, 100 Favorite Mysteries of the Century*, Mystery Reader's Journal and The Boston Herald and others. Essays:

Murder in the OPM by Leslie Ford & *Asia Rip* by George Foy.

Kate's Mystery Books, 2211 Mass Ave, Cambridge, MA
02140-1211. Phone: 617-491-2660. Email:
katesmysbks@earthlink.net. Website:
www.katesmysterybooks.com.

Jean May has worked at Murder by the Book in Portland
Oregon for fifteen years. Her tastes range from Sayers to
Lehane. She has fond memories of having chicken pox and
lying on the couch, reading one Agatha Christie after another,
while her spots faded. Essay: *Down in the Valley* by David M.
Pierce.

Murder by the Book, 3210 SE Hawthorne, Portland, OR
97214. Phone: 503-232-9995. Email: books@mbtb.com.
Website: www.mbtb.com.

Eric Mays is a former employee at Creatures 'n Crooks
Bookshoppe in Richmond, Virginia. Besides being surrounded
by books and, of course, reading them, Eric also enjoys writing.
Essay: *Pest Control* by Bill Fitzhugh.

Creatures 'n Crooks Bookshoppe, 9762 Midlothian Turnpike,
Richmond, VA 23235-4973. Phone: 804-330-4111. Email:
info@cncbooks.com. Website: www.cncbooks.com.

Mary Ann McDonald joined Capital Crimes upon its move to
Sacramento, two years ago. Cutting "mystery teeth" on Agatha
Christie at seven, reading remains a daily addiction. Lacking a
garret, a squalid apartment (with two Basenji dogs) serves as
home. Essay: *Shadow of a Broken Man* by George C. Chesbro.

Capital Crimes Mystery Bookstore, 906 Second St,
Sacramento, CA 95814. Phone: 916-441-4798. Email:
books@capitalcrimes.com. Website: www.capitalcrimes.com.

Joseph Morales. Born in New York City. Read Rex Stout as a lad. Practiced emergency medicine for 18 years. Did government administration, a much more bloody venture. Read McBain, Block, Pearson and decided to sell books instead. Ahhhh. Peace at last. Essay: *Night Dogs* by Kent Anderson.

> **Capital Crimes Mystery Bookstore**, 906 Second St, Sacramento, CA 95814. Phone: 916-441-4798. Email: books@capitalcrimes.com. Website: www.capitalcrimes.com.

Gary Warren Niebuhr is the author of *A Reader's Guide to the Private Eye Novel* and the upcoming *Make Mine A Mystery*. He is the owner of P.I.E.S., a bookselling operation that specializes in the private eye. Essay: *The Loud Adios* by Ken Kuhlken.

> **P.I.E.S.** (Private Investigator Entertainment Service). Email: piesbook@execpc.com. Website: http://www.execpc.com/~piesbook/piescatalog.html.

Susan Oleksiw is the author of the Mellingham series featuring Chief of Police Joe Silva (*Friends and Enemies*, 2001). While planning her first trip to India, she came across Agatha Christie's *They Came to Baghdad*, and discovered a kindred soul. She is also co-founder of The Larcom Press, which publishes The Larcom Review and the Larcom Mystery series. Essay: *According to the Evidence* by Henry Cecil.

> **The Larcom Press**, PO Box 161, Prides Crossing, MA 01965. Phone: 978-927-8707. Website: www.larcompress.com.

Maria Parker has been a mystery reader for more years than she cares to remember, starting with Agatha Christie in her teens. An ESL teacher in real life, she wishes she could assign mysteries for reading homework. She is a frequent contributor to The Drood Review. Essays: *Lonely Hearts* by John Harvey & *Bearing Witness* by Michael A. Kahn.

Jill of all trades, master of none until the 1989 opening of The Poisoned Pen, historian/librarian/lawyer **Barbara Peters** remains astonished at the enjoyment she gains from 90 hour weeks and at the enthusiasm of her (still original) staff. Even more fun is editing a large mystery list at Poisoned Pen Press. Essay: *A Famine of Horses* by P.F. Chisholm.

> **The Poisoned Pen**, 4014 N. Goldwater #101, Scottsdale, AZ 85251. Phone: 888-560-9919. Email: sales@poisonedpen.com. Website: www.poisonedpen.com.

Kathy Phillips is an owner, with Andy Thurnauer, of Spenser's Mystery Bookshop in Boston. She practiced law for twenty years before turning her avocation, buying and selling mysteries, into her vocation. She has written reviews for The Drood Review, Mystery Scene and The Women's Review of Books. Besides reading, she enjoys music, particularly cabaret and opera. Essays: *A Question of Guilt* by Frances Fyfield, *The Zero Trap* by Paula Gosling & *The Red, White, and Blues* by Rob Kantner.

> **Spenser's Mystery Bookshop**, 223 Newbury St, Boston, MA 02116-2568. Phone: 617-262-0880. Email: spensers@spensersmysterybooks.com. Website: www.spensersmysterybooks.com.

Sally Powers is Editor and Publisher of I Love A Mystery, an on-line newsletter reviewing mystery fiction. For twenty-five years she was a television casting director for such shows as *Hill Street Blues*, *Police Woman* and *Police Story*. Essays: *Death from the Woods* by Brigitte Aubert & *Dog in the Dark* by Gerald Hammond.

> **I Love a Mystery**, 13547 Ventura Blvd #111, Sherman Oaks, CA 91423-3825. Email: sallypowers@earthlink.net. Website: www.ILoveAMysteryNewsletter.com.

Amy Proni is a confirmed Italophile; she was stationed at Aviano. When not painting silk or felting wool, she can be found in Kalamazoo, where she managed Deadly Passions Bookshop from 1992 through 1999. She lives with her husband Tullio, a native of northern Italy, plays with a cat named Tabula Rasa and dreams about moving to the northern reaches of Michigan's Upper Peninsula. Essays: *A Comedy of Murders* by George Herman & *Death at La Fenice* by Donna Leon.

Kathleen Riley, owner of Black Bird Mysteries, could never satisfy her childhood cravings for books. Even now, surrounded by towering stacks of books, she still can't resist asking for more, please! Essays: *Before the Fact* by Francis Iles & *The Line-Up* by Helen Reilly.

> **Black Bird Mysteries**, PO Box 444, Keedysville, MD 21756-0444. Phone: 800-449-7709. Email: info@blackbird-mysteries.com. Website: www.blackbird-mysteries.com.

Until her death in December 2001, **Paige Rose** was co-owner of Mystery Loves Company. She was a mentor to many new mystery writers and enjoyed critiquing their work. She also loved professional wrestling and doing needlework. Essays: *The Christening Day Murders* by Lee Harris & *The Big Blowdown* by George P. Pelecanos.

> **Mystery Loves Company**, 1730 Fleet St, Baltimore, MD 21231-2919. Phone: 800-538-0042. Website: www.mysterylovescompany.com.

Tom & Enid Schantz have been selling, publishing, and writing about mysteries since 1970, when they began selling mysteries by mail. They have also operated a retail mystery bookstore (1980-2000) in Boulder, Colorado, published reprints of early detective fiction and Sherlockiana (1973-1979), and in 1997 launched The Rue Morgue Press, reprinting vintage mysteries (including *Common or Garden Crime*). In addition to a monthly column for The Denver Post, they write the mystery section of *What Do I Read Next?* In 2001 they received the Raven from the Mystery Writers of America. Essays: *The Paladin* by Brian Garfield & *Common or Garden Crime* by Sheila Pim.

Rue Morgue, PO Box 4119, Boulder, CO 80306. Phone: 303-443-5757. Email: tomenid@attbi.com.

Karen Spengler works as both a bookseller and a CPA, which seriously cuts into her valuable reading time. She owns I Love a Mystery, which she insists on calling "Kansas City's Mystery Bookstore," even though it is located in Mission, Kansas. Essays: *The Portland Laugher* by Earl Emerson & *The Murders of Mrs. Austin and Mrs. Beale* by Jill McGown.

I Love a Mystery, 5460 Martway, Mission, KS 66205. Phone: 913-432-2583. Email: kas@iloveamystery.net.

Kate Stine established her editing and consulting business in 1995 after many years in book publishing. Her clients have included The Mary Higgins Clark Mystery Magazine, The Mystery Writers of America, and Agatha Christie Ltd. She was also editor-in-chief of The Armchair Detective Magazine from 1992-1997. Essay: *The Seventh Sinner* by Elizabeth Peters.

Nancy-Stephanie Stone writes on espionage and lives with three greyhounds in Cambridge and Gloucester, Massachusetts. She writes for The Drood Review and other periodicals and is the author of *A Reader's Guide to the Spy and Thriller Novel* (1997). Since the Cold War ended, she will not be moving to Berlin. Essays: *Burn Season* by John Lantigua & *Mecca for Murder* by Stephen Marlowe.

Lelia Taylor is co-owner with her daughter, Annie, of Creatures 'n Crooks Bookshoppe in Richmond, Virginia. Their deep love of reading and Lelia's strong desire to leave the corporate world led to taking a chance on a dream. Essay: *Death's Favorite Child* by Frankie Y. Bailey.

> **Creatures 'n Crooks Bookshoppe**, 9762 Midlothian Turnpike, Richmond, VA 23235-4973. Phone: 804-330-4111. Email: info@cncbooks.com. Website: www.cncbooks.com.

Beth Thoenen is managing editor of The Drood Review. Essays: *Death and Other Lovers* by Jo Bannister & *Bucket Nut* by Liza Cody.

David Thompson writes: "Having worked at Murder by the Book (Houston, Texas) for thirteen years, my reading preferences have evolved to include both the hardboiled crime fiction of Randy Wayne White, George P. Pelecanos, and James Lee Burke, as well as the comic mysteries of Bill Fitzhugh, Christopher Moore and Lauren Henderson." Essay: *Dover and the Unkindest Cut of All* by Joyce Porter.

> **Murder by the Book**, 2342 Bissonnet, Houston, TX 77005-1512. Phone: 713-524-8597. Email: murderbk@swbell.net. Website: www.murderbooks.com.

Deb Tomaselli runs the Space-Crime Continuum with her husband, Chris Aylott. Sales Manager Otis the Cat keeps an eye on them both. Deb's love of mysteries began at age ten when she received her first Trixie Belden books. Essays: *A Trouble of Fools* by Linda Barnes & *The Whispering Wall* by Patricia Carlon.

> **Space-Crime Continuum**, 92 King St, Northampton, MA 01060. Phone: 413-584-0994. Email: books@spacecrime.com. Website: www.spacecrime.com.

Sharon Villines has a long and checkered history with the genre. First as a reader, then writing a research newsletter for writers, and including doing reviews and research in the history of detective fiction. Essays: *Beyond Reasonable Doubt* by C.W. Grafton & *The Leavenworth Case* by Anna Katharine Green.

Anya Weber lives in Boston, where she edits textbooks for Houghton Mifflin Company. She has been a mystery fan since discovering the Encyclopedia Brown books at the age of seven, and contributes regularly to The Drood Review. Essay: *Complicity* by Iain Banks.

Terry M. Weyna began reading mysteries as a sort of buswoman's holiday in the early days of her law practice 20 years ago. Today she lives in Sacramento, California, with the world's best man, two crazy cats and 7000 books. She is a frequent contributor to The Drood Review. Essays: *Fugitive Colors* by Margaret Maron & *The Apostrophe Thief* by Barbara Paul.

Linda Wiken, owner of Prime Crime Books in Ottawa, Canada, is a writer of published mystery short stories and non-published (as yet!) novels. Her stories have appeared in the four Ladies' Killing Circle anthologies as well as magazines. She also writes for the Ottawa Police Service newsletter and sings in their choir. Essay: *The Debt to Pleasure* by John Lanchester.

> **Prime Crime**, 891 Bank St, Ottawa, ON K1S 3W4 Canada. Phone: 613-238-2583. Email: mystery@magi.com. Website: www.infoweb.magi.com/~mystery.

Shopping list

Current US editions are listed with the publisher, ISBN and price, if available as of January 2002. Prices and availability change constantly. For help in locating copies of any of these titles, including out of print books, visit **www.mysterybooksellers.com** to find a booksellers who specializes in mysteries near you.

❏ ❏   **Catherine Aird**. *The Stately Home Murder*
       (not currently in print)

❏ ❏   **Kent Anderson**. *Night Dogs*
       (Bantam, 0553578774, $6.50)

❏ ❏   **Brigitte Aubert**. *Death from the Woods*
       (Berkley, 0425179052, $12.00)

❏ ❏   **Frankie Y. Bailey**. *Death's Favorite Child*
       (Overmountain, 1570721467, $15.00)

❏ ❏   **Iain Banks**. *Complicity*
       (not currently in print)

❏ ❏   **Jo Bannister**. *Death and Other Lovers*
       (not currently in print)

❏ ❏   **Linda Barnes**. *A Trouble of Fools*
       (Hyperion, 0786889535, $4.50)

❏ ❏   **Eleanor Taylor Bland**. *Done Wrong*
       (St. Martin's, 0312957947, $5.99)

❏ ❏   **Eleanor Boylan**. *Working Murder*
       (not currently in print)

❏ ❏   **Herbert Brean**. *Hardly a Man Is Now Alive*
       (not currently in print)

❏ ❏   **Patricia Carlon**. *The Whispering Wall*
       (Soho, 1569471118, $12.00)

❏ ❏   **Vera Caspary**. *Laura*
       (ibooks, 0743400100, $14.00)

❏ ❏   **Henry Cecil**. *According to the Evidence*
       (Academy Chicago, 0897332954, $7.95)

❏ ❏   **George C. Chesbro**. *Shadow of a Broken Man*
       (Apache Beach, 0967450373, $16.99)

❏ ❏ **Lee Child**. *Running Blind*
(Jove, 0515130974, $7.99)

❏ ❏ **P.F. Chisholm**. *A Famine of Horses*
(Poisoned Pen, 1890208272, $14.95)

❏ ❏ **Liza Cody**. *Bucket Nut*
(not currently in print)

❏ ❏ **Manning Coles**. *Without Lawful Authority*
(not currently in print)

❏ ❏ **Susan Rogers Cooper**. *The Man in the Green Chevy*
(not currently in print)

❏ ❏ **David A. Crossman**. *A Show of Hands*
(Down East Books, 089272398X, $14.95)

❏ ❏ **Stan Cutler**. *Rough Cut*
(Signet, 0451182537, $4.99)

❏ ❏ **Barbara D'Amato**. *Good Cop, Bad Cop*
(Forge, 0812590147, $6.99)

❏ ❏ **Elizabeth Daly**. *Murders in Volume 2*
(not currently in print)

❏ ❏ **Jeanne M. Dams**. *The Victim in Victoria Station*
(Worldwide, 0373263686, $5.99)

❏ ❏ **Carole Nelson Douglas**. *Irene's Last Waltz*
(not currently in print)

❏ ❏ **Ruth Dudley Edwards**. *Matricide at St. Martha's*
(Poisoned Pen Press, 1890208922, $14.95 - May '02)

❏ ❏ **Earl Emerson**. *The Portland Laugher*
(Ballantine, 0345397827, $6.50)

❏ ❏ **Loren D. Estleman**. *Jitterbug*
(Forge, 0812545370, $5.99)

❏ ❏ **Elizabeth Eyre**. *Death of the Duchess*
(not currently in print)

❏ ❏ **Terence Faherty**. *Kill Me Again*
(not currently in print)

❏ ❏ **Bill Fitzhugh**. *Pest Control*
(Avon, 0380788683, $5.99)

❏ ❏ **Leslie Ford**. *Murder in the OPM*
(not currently in print)

❏ ❏ **George Foy**. *Asia Rip*
(not currently in print)

❏ ❏ **Frances Fyfield**. *A Question of Guilt*
(not currently in print)
❏ ❏ **Brian Garfield**. *The Paladin*
(not currently in print)
❏ ❏ **Charlotte Perkins Gilman**. *Unpunished*
(Feminist Press, 1558611851, $10.95)
❏ ❏ **Dorothy Gilman**. *The Tightrope Walker*
(Fawcett, 0449211770, $6.50)
❏ ❏ **Paula Gosling**. *The Zero Trap*
(not currently in print)
❏ ❏ **C.W. Grafton**. *Beyond Reasonable Doubt*
(not currently in print)
❏ ❏ **Anna Katharine Green**. *The Leavenworth Case*
(not currently in print)
❏ ❏ **Jane Haddam**. *Not a Creature Was Stirring*
(not currently in print)
❏ ❏ **Gerald Hammond**. *Dog in the Dark*
(not currently in print)
❏ ❏ **Cyril Hare**. *With a Bare Bodkin*
(not currently in print)
❏ ❏ **Joseph Harrington**. *The Last Known Address*
(not currently in print)
❏ ❏ **Lee Harris**. *The Christening Day Murders*
(Fawcett, 0449148718, $5.99)
❏ ❏ **Jamie Harrison**. *The Edge of the Crazies*
(St. Martin's, 0312959427, $5.99)
❏ ❏ **John Harvey**. *Lonely Hearts*
(Henry Holt, 0805054944, $11.00)
❏ ❏ **George Herman**. *A Comedy of Murders*
(not currently in print)
❏ ❏ **Georgette Heyer**. *Envious Casca*
(not currently in print)
❏ ❏ **William Hjortsberg**. *Falling Angel*
(St. Martin's, 0312957955, $5.99)
❏ ❏ **Wendy Hornsby**. *Midnight Baby*
(Signet, 0451181360, $5.99)
❏ ❏ **Barry Hughart**. *Bridge of Birds*
(Ballantine, 0345321383, $6.99)

❑ ❑ **Francis Iles**. *Before the Fact*
(Amereon, 0848801717, $25.95)

❑ ❑ **Bill James**. *Panicking Ralph*
(Norton, 0393323064, $7.95)

❑ ❑ **Michael A. Kahn**. *Bearing Witness*
(Forge, 0312848838, $23.95)

❑ ❑ **Rob Kantner**. *The Red, White, and Blues*
(not currently in print)

❑ ❑ **Mary Anne Kelly**. *Park Lane South, Queens*
(not currently in print)

❑ ❑ **William Kent Krueger**. *Iron Lake*
(Pocket, 0671016970, $6.99)

❑ ❑ **Ken Kuhlken**. *The Loud Adios*
(not currently in print)

❑ ❑ **John Lanchester**. *The Debt to Pleasure*
(Picador, 0312420366, $13.00)

❑ ❑ **Joe R. Lansdale**. *The Nightrunners*
(Carroll & Graf, 0786702893, $4.95)

❑ ❑ **John Lantigua**. *Burn Season*
(not currently in print)

❑ ❑ **Robert Leininger**. *Killing Suki Flood*
(Trafalgar Square, 1874061157, $11.00)

❑ ❑ **Donna Leon**. *Death at La Fenice*
(HarperPaperbacks, 0061043370, $6.99)

❑ ❑ **Gaston Leroux**. *The Mystery of the Yellow Room*
(Buccaneer, 0899661416, $27.95)

❑ ❑ **Philip MacDonald**. *Warrant for X*
(not currently in print)

❑ ❑ **John Malcolm**. *A Back Room in Somers Town*
(not currently in print)

❑ ❑ **Stephen Marlowe**. *Mecca for Murder*
(not currently in print)

❑ ❑ **Margaret Maron**. *Fugitive Colors*
(Warner, 0446403938, $5.99)

❑ ❑ **Archer Mayor**. *Borderlines*
(Warner, 0446404438, $6.99)

❑ ❑ **Robert R. McCammon**. *Boy's Life*
(Pocket, 0671743058, $7.99)

❑ ❑ **Jill McGown**. *The Murders of Mrs. Austin and Mrs. Beale* (Fawcett, 0449221628, $6.50)

❑ ❑ **Sean McGrady**. *Dead Letters* (Pocket, 0671742671, $4.99)

❑ ❑ **Marcia Muller & Bill Pronzini**. *Beyond the Grave* (Carroll & Graf, 0786706503, $5.95)

❑ ❑ **Barbara Neely**. *Blanche Cleans Up* (Penguin, 0140277471, $5.99)

❑ ❑ **Kem Nunn**. *The Dogs of Winter* (Washington Square, 0671793349, $14.00)

❑ ❑ **Anthony Oliver**. *The Pew Group* (not currently in print)

❑ ❑ **Marco Page**. *Fast Company* (not currently in print)

❑ ❑ **Barbara Paul**. *The Apostrophe Thief* (not currently in print)

❑ ❑ **George P. Pelecanos**. *The Big Blowdown* (St. Martin's, 0312242913, $14.95)

❑ ❑ **Thomas Perry**. *The Butcher's Boy* (not currently in print)

❑ ❑ **Elizabeth Peters**. *The Seventh Sinner* (Warner, 0445407786, $6.99)

❑ ❑ **David M. Pierce**. *Down in the Valley* (not currently in print)

❑ ❑ **Sheila Pim**. *Common or Garden Crime* (Rue Morgue, 0915230364, $14.00)

❑ ❑ **Joyce Porter**. *Dover and the Unkindest Cut of All* (Foul Play, 0881501743, $5.95)

❑ ❑ **Richard S. Prather**. *The Wailing Frail* (not currently in print)

❑ ❑ **Bill Pronzini**. *Shackles* (not currently in print)

❑ ❑ **Derek Raymond**. *I Was Dora Suarez* (not currently in print)

❑ ❑ **Philip Reed**. *Bird Dog* (Pocket, 0671001655, $6.50)

❑ ❑ **Helen Reilly**. *The Line-Up* (not currently in print)

❏ ❏ **Robert Richardson**. *The Latimer Mercy*
(not currently in print)
❏ ❏ **Mary Roberts Rinehart**. *The Man in Lower Ten*
(not currently in print)
❏ ❏ **Jean Ruryk**. *Chicken Little Was Right*
(not currently in print)
❏ ❏ **Alan Russell**. *The Hotel Detective*
(not currently in print)
❏ ❏ **Walter Satterthwait**. *Wilde West*
(not currently in print)
❏ ❏ **John Shannon**. *The Concrete River*
(not currently in print)
❏ ❏ **Seymour Shubin**. *Never Quite Dead*
(not currently in print)
❏ ❏ **Mary Stewart**. *Nine Coaches Waiting*
(Harper, 0380820765, $7.99)
❏ ❏ **Alice Tilton**. *The Left Leg*
(not currently in print)
❏ ❏ **Colin Watson**. *Just What the Doctor Ordered*
(not currently in print)
❏ ❏ **Hillary Waugh**. *Sleep Long, My Love*
(not currently in print)
❏ ❏ **Donald E. Westlake**. *Kahawa*
(not currently in print)
❏ ❏ **Don Winslow**. *A Cool Breeze on the Underground*
(St. Martin's, 0312958641, $6.50)

About the editor

Since 1982, Jim Huang has edited and published The Drood Review, a bimonthly mystery review newsletter, which he founded with fellow alums of Swarthmore College. His essays have also appeared in *100 Great Detectives, The St. James Guide to Crime and Mystery Writers*, Pomp and Circumstantial Evidence newsletter, and elsewhere.

Jim is also the proprietor of Deadly Passions Bookshop, formerly of Kalamazoo, Michigan, and now online at **www.deadlypassions.com**. Jim served as director of the Independent Mystery Booksellers Association from 1997 through 2001.

In 2000, Jim moved to Indiana, with his wife, Jennie Jacobson, and their daughters, Grace and Miranda (who enjoy uncovering the solutions to mysteries just as much as their parents), where he also enjoys coaching first-grade soccer.

About Drood Review Books

They Died in Vain is A Drood Review Book published by The Crum Creek Press. Previous press publications include *100 Favorite Mysteries of the Century: Selected by the Independent Mystery Booksellers Association*, which won the Agatha and Anthony Awards for Best Nonfiction of 2000.

Drood Review Books is the book publishing affiliate of The Drood Review, a bimonthly newsletter that reviews and previews new mysteries. The newsletter celebrates its twentieth anniversary in 2002.

For more information, visit **www.droodreview.com** or write:

The Drood Review
484 East Carmel Drive #378
Carmel, IN 46032